Acclaim for Julian Barnes's

# Pulse

"Barnes is among the most adventurous writers—in style, versatility and narrative structure—of his Amis-McEwan-Hitchens generation."          —*The New York Times Book Review*

"A moving and truth-telling work of fiction."
                                        —*The Boston Globe*

"Of our leading novelists, Julian Barnes has one of the richest historical imaginations. . . . His stories tend to be quietly observational, rather traditional in manner, and his characters are never tragic. They are inhabitants of a gray-scale world, plugging on through life chastened by the experiences Barnes recounts, but not devastated by them. That may be why we identify with them so easily."          —*Los Angeles Times*

"Full of the sidelong wit and intelligence that make the writer one of our most consistently deft short-form stylists. . . . [A] quietly remarkable, elegant book."     —*The Telegraph* (London)

"A book that is almost entirely masterly. . . . These stories are acutely observational. They neither satirize the speakers, nor celebrate them. They make art out of the quotidian details of modern conversation—and they are very funny."
                                        —*The Denver Post*

"A collection of stories that engages the reader's intellect and heart, the best of fiction's traditional concerns."
                                        —*Pittsburgh Post-Gazette*

4/14

"In *Pulse*, Julian Barnes is as perceptive and intelligent as in any other of his dazzling novels and nonfiction, and, it must be said, fully as serious. . . . The reader appreciates Barnes's unflinching realism and his determination to boil life down to its essence, however disconcerting that process may be."
—*Providence Journal*

"Sharply elegant, piercing investigation of relationships."
—*Vogue*

"Barnes is a master at establishing the intimacies of mortality in this kind of relationship, forever testing the limits to which our faith in human connection might stretch."
—*The Observer* (London)

Julian Barnes

# Pulse

Julian Barnes is the author of two previous story collections, *Cross Channel* and *The Lemon Table*, and fourteen other books. He was awarded the Man Booker Prize for his novel *The Sense of an Ending*. He lives in London.

www.julianbarnes.com

VINTAGE

INTERNATIONAL

# Pulse

Stories

Julian Barnes

*Vintage International*
Vintage Books
A Division of Random House, Inc.
New York

FIRST VINTAGE INTERNATIONAL EDITION, FEBRUARY 2012

Some of the stories in this work were previously published in slightly
different form in the following: "Harmony" and "Marriage Lines" in *Granta*;
"At Phil and Joanna's I: 60/40" and "Sleeping with John Updike" in
the *Guardian*; "Complicity," "East Wind," "The Limner," and "Trespass" in
*The New Yorker*; and "At Phil and Joanna's 2: Marmalade" in *The Sunday Times*.

The Library of Congress has cataloged the Knopf edition as follows:
Barnes, Julian.
Pulse / Julian Barnes.—1st American ed.
p. cm.
1. Title.
PR6052.A6657P85 2011
823'.914—dc22    2011002736

**Vintage ISBN: 978-0-307-74240-7**

Book design by Michael Appuhn

www.vintagebooks.com

Printed in the United States of America
10  9  8  7  6  5  4  3  2  1

for Pat

# Contents

# One

# East Wind

THE PREVIOUS November, a row of wooden beach huts, their paintwork lifted and flaked by the hard east wind, had burnt to the ground. The fire brigade came from twelve miles away, and had nothing to do by the time it arrived. Yobs on Rampage, the local paper decided; though no culprit was ever found. An architect from a more fashionable part of the coastline told the regional TV news that the huts were part of the town's social heritage, and must be rebuilt. The council announced that it would consider all options, but since then had done nothing.

Vernon had moved to the town only a few months before, and had no feelings about the beach huts. If anything, their disappearance improved the view from the Right Plaice, where he sometimes had lunch. From a window table he now looked out across a strip of concrete to damp shingle, a bored sky and a lifeless sea. That was the east coast: for months on end you got bits of bad weather and lots of no weather. This was fine by him: he'd moved here to have no weather in his life.

"You are done?"

He didn't look up at the waitress. "All the way from the Urals," he said, still gazing at the long, flat sea.

"Pardon?"

"Nothing between here and the Urals. That's where the wind comes from. Nothing to stop it. Straight across all those countries." Cold enough to freeze your knob off, he might have added in other circumstances.

"*Oorals*," she repeated. As he caught the accent, he looked up at her. A broad face, streaked hair, chunky body, and not doing any waitressy number in hope of a bigger tip. Must be one of those Eastern Europeans who were all over the country nowadays. Building trade, pubs and restaurants, fruit picking. Came over here in vans and coaches, lived in rabbit warrens, made themselves a bit of money. Some stayed, some went home. Vernon didn't mind one way or the other. That's what he found more often than not these days: he didn't mind one way or the other.

"Are you from one of them?"

"One of what?"

"One of those countries. Between here and the Urals."

"*Oorals*. Yes, perhaps."

That was an odd answer, he thought. Or maybe her sense of geography wasn't so strong.

"Fancy a swim?"

"A swim?"

"Yes, you know. Swim. Splash splash, front crawl, breaststroke."

"No swim."

"Fine," he said. He hadn't meant it anyway. "Bill, please."

As he waited, he looked back across the concrete to the damp shingle. A beach hut had recently sold for twenty grand. Or was it thirty? Somewhere down on the south coast. Spiralling house prices, the market going mad: that's what the papers said. Not that it touched this part of the country, or the property he dealt in. The market had bottomed out here long ago, the graph as horizontal as the sea. Old people died, you sold their flats and houses to people who in their turn would get old in them and then die. That was a lot of his trade. The town wasn't fashionable, never had been: Londoners carried on up the A12 to somewhere pricier. Fine by him. He'd lived in London all his life until the divorce. Now he had a quiet job, a rented flat, and saw the kids every other weekend. When they got older, they'd probably be bored with this place and start acting the little snobs. But for the moment they liked the sea, throwing pebbles into it, eating chips.

When she brought the bill, he said, "We could run away together and live in a beach hut."

"I do not think," she replied, shaking her head, as if she assumed he meant it. Oh well, the old English sense of humour, takes a while for people to get used to it.


He had a few rentals to attend to—changes of tenancy, redecoration, damp problems—and then a sale up the coast, so he didn't return to the Right Plaice for a few weeks. He ate his haddock and mushies, and read the paper. There was some town in Lincolnshire which was suddenly half Polish, there'd been so many immigrants. Nowadays, more Catholics went to church on Sundays than Anglicans, they were saying, what with all these Eastern Europeans. He didn't mind one way or the other. Actually, he liked the Poles he'd met—brickies, plasterers, electricians. Good workers, well trained, did what they said, trustworthy. It was time the good old British building trade had a kick up the arse, Vernon thought.

The sun was out that day, slanting low across the sea, annoying his eyes. Late March, and bits of spring were getting even to this part of the coast.

"How about that swim, then?" he asked as she brought the bill.

"Oh no. No swim."

"I'm guessing you might be Polish."

"My name is Andrea," she replied.

"Not that I mind whether you're Polish or not."

"I do not also."

The thing was, he'd never been much good at flirting; never quite said the right thing. And since the divorce, he'd got worse at it, if that was possible, because his heart wasn't in it. Where was his heart? Question for another day. Today's subject: flirting. He knew all too well the look in a woman's eye when you didn't get it right. Where's *he* coming from, the look said. Anyway, it took two to flirt. And maybe he was getting too old for it. Thirty-seven, father of two, Gary (8) and Melanie (5). That's how the papers would put it if he was washed up on the coast some morning.

"I'm an estate agent," he said. That was another line which often hampered flirting.

"What is this?"

"I sell houses. And flats. And we do rentals. Rooms, flats, houses."

"Is it interesting?"

"It's a living."

"We all need living."

He suddenly thought: no, you can't flirt either. Maybe you can flirt in your own language, but you can't do it in English, so we're even. He also thought: she looks sturdy. Maybe I need someone sturdy. She might be my age, for all I know. Not that he minded one way or the other. He wasn't going to ask her out.

He asked her out. There wasn't much choice of "out" in this town. One cinema, a few pubs, and the couple of other restaurants where she didn't work. Apart from that, there was bingo for the old people whose flats he would sell after they were dead, and a club where some halfhearted goths loitered. Kids drove into

Colchester on a Friday night and bought enough drugs to see them through the weekend. No wonder they burnt down the beach huts.

He liked her at first for what she wasn't. She wasn't flirty, she wasn't gabby, she wasn't pushy. She didn't mind that he was an estate agent, or that he was divorced with two kids. Other women had taken a quick look and said: no. He reckoned women were more attracted to men who were still in a marriage, however fucked up it was, than to ones picking up the pieces afterwards. Not surprising really. But Andrea didn't mind all that. Didn't ask questions much. Didn't answer them either, for that matter. The first time they kissed, he thought of asking if she was really Polish, but then he forgot.

He suggested his place, but she refused. She said she'd come next time. He spent an anxious few days wondering what it would be like to go to bed with someone different after so long. He drove fifteen miles up the coast to buy condoms where no one knew him. Not that he was ashamed, or embarrassed; just didn't want anyone knowing, or guessing, his business.

"This is a nice apartment."

"Well, if an estate agent can't find himself a decent flat, what's the world coming to?"

She had an overnight bag with her; she took off her clothes in the bathroom and came back in a nightdress. They climbed into bed and he turned out the light. She felt very tense to him. He felt very tense to himself.

"We could just cuddle," he suggested.

"What is cuddle?"

He demonstrated.

"So cuddle is not fucking?"

"No, cuddle is not fucking."

"OK, cuddle."

After that they relaxed, and she soon fell asleep.

The next time, after some kissing, he reacquainted himself

with the lubricated struggle of the condom. He knew he was meant to unroll it, but found himself trying to tug it on like a sock, pulling at the rim in a haphazard way. Doing it in the dark didn't help either. But she didn't say anything, or cough discouragingly, and eventually he turned towards her. She pulled up her nightie and he climbed on top of her. His mind was half filled with lust and fucking, and half empty, as if wondering what he was up to. He didn't think about her very much that first time. It was a question of looking out for yourself. Later you could look out for the other person.

"Was that OK?" he said after a while.

"Yes, was OK."

Vernon laughed in the dark.

"Are you laughing at me? Was not OK for you?"

"Andrea," he said, "everything's OK. Nobody's laughing at you. I won't let anyone laugh at you." As she slept, he thought: we're starting again, both of us. I don't know what she's had in her past, but maybe we're both starting again from the same sort of low point, and that's OK. Everything's OK.

The next time she was more relaxed, and gripped him hard with her legs. He couldn't tell whether she came or not.

"Gosh you're strong," he said afterwards.

"Is strong bad?"

"No, no. Not at all. Strong's good."

But the next time he noticed that she didn't grip him so hard. She didn't much like him playing with her breasts either. No, that was unfair. She didn't seem to mind if he did or didn't. Or rather, if he wanted to, that was fine, but it was for him, not for her. That's what he understood, anyway. And who said you had to talk about everything in the first week?

He was glad neither of them was any good at flirting: it was a kind of deception. Whereas Andrea was never anything but straight with him. She didn't talk much, but what she said was what she did. She would meet him where and when he asked, and be standing there, looking out for him, brushing a streak of hair out of her eyes, holding on to her bag more firmly than was necessary in this town.

"You're as reliable as a Polish builder," he told her one day.

"Is that good?"

"That's very good."

"Is English expression?"

"It is now."

She asked him to correct her English when she made a mistake. He got her to say "I don't think so" instead of "I do not think"; but actually, he preferred the way she talked. He always understood her, and those phrases which weren't quite right seemed part of her. Maybe he didn't want her talking like an Englishwoman in case she started behaving like an Englishwoman—well, like one in particular. And anyway, he didn't want to play the teacher.

It was the same in bed. Things are what they are, he said to himself. If she always wore a nightie, perhaps it was a Catholic thing—not that she ever mentioned going to church. If he asked her to do stuff to him, she did it, and seemed to enjoy it; but she didn't ask him to do stuff back to her—didn't even seem to like his hand down there much. But this didn't bother him; she was allowed to be who she was.

She never asked him in. If he dropped her off, she'd be trotting up the concrete path before he'd got the hand brake on; if he picked her up, she'd already be outside, waiting. At first this was fine, then it began to feel a bit odd, so he asked to see where she lived, just for a minute, so he could imagine where she was when she wasn't with him. They went back into the house—1930s semi, pebbledash, multioccupation, metal window frames rusting up badly—and she opened her door. His professional eye took in the dimensions, furnishings, and probable rental cost; his lover's eye took in a small dressing table with photos in plastic frames and a picture of the Virgin. There was a single bed, tiny sink, rubbish microwave, small TV, and clothes on hangers clipped precariously to the picture rail. Something in him was touched by seeing her life exposed like that in the minute or so before they stepped outside again. To cover this sudden emotion, Vernon said,

"You shouldn't be paying more than fifty-five. Plus services. I can get you somewhere bigger for the same price."

"Is OK."

Now that spring was here, they went for drives into Suffolk and looked at English things: half-timbered houses with no damp courses, thatched roofs which put you in a higher insurance band. They stopped by a village green and he sat down on a bench overlooking a pond, but she didn't fancy that so they looked at the church instead. He hoped she wouldn't ask him to explain the difference between Anglicans and Catholics—or the history behind it all. Something about Henry the Eighth wanting to get married again. The king's knob. All sorts of things came down to sex if you looked at them closely enough. But happily she didn't ask.

She began to take his arm, and to smile more easily. He gave her the key to his flat; tentatively, she started leaving overnight stuff there. One Sunday, in the dark, he reached across to the bedside drawer and found he was out of condoms. He swore, and had to explain.

"Is OK."

"No, Andrea, is bloody not OK. Last thing I need is you getting pregnant."

"I do not think so. Not get pregnant. Is OK."

He trusted her. Later, as she slept, he wondered what exactly she had meant. That she couldn't have kids? Or that she was taking something herself, to make doubly sure? If so, what would the Virgin Mary have to say about that? Let's hope she isn't relying on the rhythm method, he suddenly thought. Guaranteed to fail on a regular basis and keep the pope as happy as Larry.

Time passed; she met Gary and Melanie; they took to her. She didn't tell them what to do; they told her, and she went along with it. They also asked her questions he'd never dared, or cared, to ask.

"Andrea, are you married?"

"Can we watch TV as long as we like?"

"Were you married?"

"If I ate three would I be sick?"

"Why aren't you married?"

"How old are you?"

"What team do you support?"

"You got any children?"

"Are you and Dad getting married?"

He learnt the answers to some of these questions—like any sensible woman, she wasn't telling her age. One night, in the dark, after he'd delivered the kids back, and was too upset for sex, as he always was on these occasions, he said, "Do you think you could love me?"

"Yes, I think I would love you."

"Is that a would or a could?"

"What is the difference?"

He paused. "There's no difference. I'll take either. I'll take both. I'll take whatever you've got to give."


He didn't know why it started, the next bit. Because he was beginning to fall in love with her, or because he didn't really want to? Or wanted to, but was afraid? Or was it that, deep down,

he had an urge to fuck everything up? That's what his wife—
ex-wife—had said to him one morning over breakfast. "Look,
Vernon, I don't hate you, I really don't. I just can't live with you
because you always fuck things up." Her statement seemed to
come out of the blue. True, he snored a bit, and dropped his
clothes where he shouldn't, and watched the normal amount of
sport on TV. But he came home on time, loved his kids, didn't
chase other women. In some people's eyes, that was the same as
fucking things up.

"Can I ask you something?"

"For sure."

"No, 'for sure' is American. English is 'yes.'"

She looked at him, as if to say, Why are you now correcting
my English?

"Yes," she repeated.

"When I didn't have a condom and you said it was OK, did
you mean it was OK then or OK always?"

"OK always."

"Blimey, do you know what a twelve-pack costs?"

That had been the wrong thing to say, even he could see that.
Christ, maybe she'd had some terrible abortion, or been raped or
something.

"So you can't have children?"

"No. Do you hate me?"

"Andrea, for God's sake." He took her hand. "I've got two kids
already. Point is, is it OK with you?"

She looked down. "No. Is not OK with me. It makes me very
unhappy."

"Well, we could . . . I don't know, see the doctor. See an
expert." He imagined the experts over here were more clued-up.

"No, no expert. NO EXPERT."

"Fine, no experts." He thought: adoption? But can I afford
another, with my outgoings?

He stopped buying condoms. He started asking questions, as tactfully as he could. But tact was like flirting: either you had it, or you didn't. No, that wasn't right. It was just easier to be tactful if you didn't care if you knew things or not; harder when you cared.

"Why are you now asking these questions?"

"Am I?"

"Yes, I think so."

"Sorry."

But he was mainly sorry that she'd noticed. Also sorry that he wouldn't stop. Couldn't stop. When they first got together, he liked the fact that he didn't know anything about her; it made things different, fresher. Gradually, she'd learnt about him, while he hadn't learnt about her. Why not continue like that? *Because you always fuck things up*, his wife, ex-wife, whispered. No, he didn't accept that. If you fall in love, you want to know. Good, bad, indifferent. Not that you're looking for bad things. That's just what falling in love means, Vernon said to himself. Or thinking about falling in love. Anyway, Andrea was a nice person, he was certain about that. So what was wrong with finding out about a nice person behind her back?

They all knew him at the Right Plaice: Mrs. Ridgewell the manageress, Jill the other waitress, and old Herbert, who owned the restaurant but only dropped in when he fancied a free bite. Vernon chose a time when the lunch trade was starting, and walked past the counter towards the toilets. The room—more of a cupboard, really—where the staff left their coats and bags was just opposite the gents. Vernon went in, found Andrea's bag, took her keys, and came back out flapping his hands as if to say, That whirry old hand-drier never quite does the trick, does it?

He winked at Andrea, walked to the hardware shop, complained about clients who had only one set of keys, strolled around for a bit, picked up the new set, went back to the Right Plaice, prepared a line about the chilly weather playing havoc with his bladder, didn't need to use it, put her keys back, and ordered a cappuccino.

The first time he went, it was the sort of drizzly afternoon when no one looks at anyone who's passing. A chap in a raincoat goes up a concrete path to a front door with frosted glass panels. Inside, he opens another door, sits on a bed, gets up suddenly, smooths out the dent in the bed, turns, sees the microwave isn't rubbish actually, puts his hand under the pillow, feels one of her nightdresses, looks at the clothes hanging from the picture rail, touches a dress she hasn't worn before, deliberately doesn't let himself look at the pictures on the little dressing table, sees himself out, locks up behind him. No one did anything wrong, did they?

The second time, he examined the Virgin Mary and the half dozen pictures. He didn't pick anything up, just went down on his haunches and looked at the photos in their plastic frames. That must be Mum, he thought, looking at the tight perm and big glasses. And there's little Andrea, all blond and a bit chubby. And is that a brother or a boyfriend? And here's somebody's birthday with so many faces you can't tell who's important and who isn't. He looked again at the six- or seven-year-old Andrea— just a bit older than Melanie—and took the image home in his head.

The third time, he eased open the top drawer; it stuck, and Andrea's mum toppled over. There was mainly underwear, most of it familiar. Then he went to the bottom drawer, because that's where secrets are normally kept, and found only sweaters and a couple of scarves. But in the middle drawer, under some shirts, were three items he laid on the bed in the same order, and even the same distance apart, as he found them. On the right was a medal, in the middle a photo framed in metal, on the left a passport. The photo showed four girls in a swimming pool, their arms round one another, a lane divider with cork floats separating one pair from the other. They were all smiling up at the camera, and had wrinkles in their white rubber caps. He instantly picked out Andrea, second from the left. The medal showed a swimmer diving into a pool, with some lines of German writing on the back and a date, 1986. How old would she have been then—eighteen, twenty? The passport confirmed it: date of birth 1967, which made her forty. It said she was born in Halle, so she was German.

And that was that. No diary, no letters, no vibrator. No secrets. He was in love—no, he was thinking about being in love—with a woman who had once won a swimming medal. Where was the harm in knowing that? Not that she swam anymore. And now he remembered it, she'd got all jumpy at the beach when Gary and Melanie made her go to the water's edge and started splashing around. Maybe she didn't want to be reminded. Or perhaps it was quite different, swimming in a competition pool versus having a dip in the sea. Like ballet dancers not wanting to do the sort of dancing everyone else did.

That evening he was deliberately jolly when they met, even a bit silly, but she seemed to notice, so he stopped. After a bit, he felt normal again. Almost normal, anyway. When he'd first started going out with girls, he found there were moments when he suddenly thought: I don't understand anything at all. With Karen, for instance: they'd been jogging along nicely, no pressure, having fun, when she'd asked, "So where's all this leading, then?" As if there were only two choices: up the aisle, or up the garden path. Other times, with other women, you'd say something, just something ordinary, and—splash—you were in deep water.

They were in bed, Andrea's nightie pulled up around her waist in the fat roll he was quite used to feeling against his belly, and he was going it a bit, when she shifted her legs and crushed him with them, like a nutcracker, he thought.

"Mmm, big strong swimmer's legs," he muttered.

She didn't answer, but he knew she'd heard. He carried on, but could tell from her body that her mind wasn't on things. Afterwards, they lay on their backs, and he said some stuff, but she didn't pick up on anything. Oh well, work tomorrow, thought Vernon. He went to sleep.

When he dropped by the Right Plaice the next evening to pick Andrea up, Mrs. Ridgewell said she'd called in sick. He rang her mobile but she didn't answer, so he texted her. Then he went round to the house and tried her bell. He left it a couple of hours, phoned again, rang the bell, then let himself in.

Her room was quite neat, and quite empty. No clothes on the picture rail, no photos on the little dressing table. Something made him open the microwave and look inside; all he saw was the circular plate. On the bed were two envelopes, one for the landlord, with keys and money inside by the feel of it, the other for Mrs. Ridgewell. Nothing for him.

Mrs. Ridgewell asked if they'd had a quarrel. No, he said, they never quarrelled.

"She was a nice girl," said the manageress. "Very reliable."

"Like a Polish builder."

"I hope you didn't say that to her. It's not a nice remark. And I don't think she was Polish."

"No, she wasn't." He looked out to sea. "*Oorals*," he found himself saying.

"Pardon?"

You went to the station and showed a photograph of the missing woman to the booking clerk, who remembered her face and told you where she'd bought a ticket to. That's what they did in films. But the nearest station was twelve miles away, and it didn't have a ticket office, just a machine you put money or plastic into. And he didn't even have a picture of her. They'd never done that thing couples do, crowding into a booth together, the girl sitting on the man's lap, both half silly and out of focus. They were probably too old for that anyway.

At home he Googled Andrea Morgen and got 497,000 results. Then he refined the question and cut the results down to 393. Did he want to search for "Andrea Morgan"? No, he didn't want to search for someone else. Most of the stuff was in German, and he scrolled through it helplessly. He'd never done languages at school, never needed them since. Then he had a thought. He looked up an online dictionary and found the German for swimmer. It was a different word if you were a man or a woman. He typed in "Andrea Morgen," "1967," "Halle," and "Schwimmerin."

Eight results, all in German. Two seemed to be from newspapers, one from an official report. And there was a picture of her. The same one he'd found in the drawer: there she was, second from the left, arms around her teammates, big wrinkles in her white swimming cap. He paused, then hit "Translate this page." Later, he found links to other pages, this time in English.

How could he have known, he asked himself. He could barely understand the science and wasn't interested in the politics. But he could understand, and was interested in, things he wished afterwards he'd never read about, things which, even as he looked out at the sea from a window table in the Right Plaice, were already beginning to change his memory of her.

Halle was in what used to be East Germany. There had been a state recruiting scheme. Girls were picked out when they were as young as eleven. Vernon tried to put together the probable life of that chubby little blond girl. Her parents signing a consent form and a secrecy form. Andrea enrolled in the Child and Youth Sports School, then in the Dynamo Sports Club in East Berlin. She had school lessons, but was mostly trained to swim and swim. It was a great honour to be a member of the Dynamo: that was why she'd had to leave home. Blood was taken from her earlobe to test how fit she was. There were pink pills and blue pills—vitamins, she was told. Later, there were injections—just more vitamins. Except that they were anabolic steroids and testosterone. It was forbidden to refuse. The training motto was "You eat the pills or you die." The coaches made sure she swallowed them.

She didn't die. Other things happened instead. Muscles grew but tendons didn't, so tendons snapped. There were sudden bursts of acne, a deepening of the voice, an increase of hair on the face and body; sometimes the pubic hair grew up over the stomach, even above the navel. There was retarded growth and problems with fertility. Vernon had to look up terms like "virilisation" and "clitoral hypertrophy," then wished he hadn't. He didn't need to look up heart disease, liver disease, deformed children, blind children.

They doped the girls because it worked. East German swimmers won medals everywhere, the women especially. Not that Andrea had got to that level. When the Berlin Wall came down and the scandal broke, when they put the poisoners—trainers, doctors, bureaucrats—on trial, her name wasn't even mentioned. In spite of the pills, she hadn't made the national team. The others, the ones who went public about what had been done to their bodies and minds, at least had gold medals and a few years of fame to show for it. Andrea had come out with nothing more than a relay medal at some forgotten championship in a country that no longer existed.

Vernon looked out at the concrete strip and the shingle beach, at the grey sea and the grey sky beyond. The view was pretending it had always been the same, for as long as people had sat at this café window. Except that there used to be a row of beach huts blocking the view. Then someone had burnt them down.

# At Phil & Joanna's 1:
# 60/40

IT WAS the week Hillary Clinton finally conceded. The table was a clutter of bottles and glasses; and though hunger had been satisfied, some mild social addiction kept making hands reach out to snaffle another grape, crumble a landslip from the cliff-face of cheese, or pick a chocolate from the box. We had talked about Obama's chances against McCain, and whether in recent weeks Hillary had demonstrated guts or mere self-deception. We had also considered whether the Labour Party was any longer distinguishable from the Conservatives, the suitability of London's streets for bendy buses, the likelihood of an al-Qaida attack on the 2012 Olympics, and the effect of global warming on English viticulture. Joanna, who had been quiet during these last two topics, now said with a sigh,

"You know, I could really do with a cigarette."

Everyone seemed to exhale slightly.

"It's just on occasions like this, isn't it?"

"The food. That lamb, by the way . . ."

"Thanks. It's six hours. Best way to do it. And star anise."

"And the wine . . ."

"Not forgetting the company."

"When I was giving up, it was the disapproval I hated more than anything. You'd ask if anyone minded, and they all said no, but you could sense them turning away and not breathing in. And either pitying you, which was patronising, or even kind of loathing you."

"And there would never be an ashtray in the house and they'd do a long, exaggerated hunt for some old saucer which had lost its cup."

"And the next stage was going outside and freezing to death."

"And if you stubbed it out in some plant pot they'd look at you as if you'd given a geranium cancer."

"I used to take my butts home in my purse. In a plastic bag."

"Like dog crap. When did that start, by the way? About the same time? People walking around with inverted plastic bags on their hands, waiting for their dogs to crap."

"I always think it must be warm, mustn't it? Feeling warm dog crap through the plastic."

"Dick, *really*."

"Well, I've never seen them waiting for it to cool down, have you?"

"These chocolates, to change the subject. Why do the drawings never match what's in the box?"

"Or is it the other way round?"

"The other way round's the same way round. They still don't match."

"The pictures are only an approximation. Like a communist menu. What would exist in an ideal world. Think of them as a metaphor."

"The chocolates?"

"No, the drawings."

"I used to love a cigar. It didn't have to be a whole one. Half would do."

"They gave you different cancers, didn't they?"

"What did?"

"Cigarettes, pipes, cigars. Didn't pipes give you lip cancer?"

"What did cigars give you?"

"Oh, the poshest kind."

"What's a posh cancer? Isn't that a contradiction in terms?"

"Bum cancer's got to be the bottom of the pile."

"Dick, *really*."

"Did I say something?"

"Cancer of the heart—is that possible?"

"Only as a metaphor, I'd say."

"George the Sixth—was that lung?"

"Or throat?"

"Anyway, it proved he had the common touch, didn't it? Like staying in Buckingham Palace and getting bombed, and going round the East End shaking hands in the rubble."

"So getting a common form of cancer was in line with that—is that what you're saying?"

"I don't know what I'm saying."

"I don't think he would have shaken hands. Being king."

"Here's a serious question. Obama, McCain, Clinton: which of the three of them was the last to smoke?"

"Bill or Hillary?"

"Hillary, of course."

"Because we all remember Bill's use of a cigar."

"Yes, but did he smoke it afterwards?"

"Or keep it in a special humidor like she kept the dress?"

"He could auction it to pay Hillary's campaign debts."

"McCain must have smoked when he was a POW."

"Obama must have had a joint or two."

"I bet Hillary never inhaled."

"By their smoking shall ye know them."

"Actually—as your token American present—Obama used to be a big smoker. Took to Nicorettes when he decided to run. But—fallen off the wagon, I hear."

"That's my man."

"Would anyone care if one of them did something bad in that line? And got photographed?"

"It would depend on the quality and nature of the contrition."

"Like Hugh Grant after getting a blow job in his car."

"Now *she* inhaled."

"*Dick*, stop it. Remove that bottle from in front of him."

"'The quality and nature of the contrition'—I like that."

"Not that Bush apologised for having been a cokehead."

"Well, he wasn't endangering others."

"Course he was."

"You mean, like passive smoking? I don't think there's passive coke inhalation, is there?"

"Not unless you sneeze."

"So there are no harmful effects on others?"

"Apart from them having to listen to tediously self-excited conversation."

"*Actually* . . ."

"Yes?"

"If Bush was, as they say, an alkie and a cokehead in his former existence, then that would help explain his presidency."

"You mean, brain damage?"

"No, the absolutism of the recovering addict."

"You *are* coming out with the phrases tonight."

"Well, it's my trade."

"The absolutism of the recovering addict. Sorry about that, Baghdad."

"So what we're saying is, it *does* make a difference what they smoked."

"Cigars used to make me mellow."

"Cigarettes used to give me such a high sometimes, my legs would tingle."

"Oh, I remember that."

"I knew someone who would set an alarm clock so he could wake up and have one in the middle of the night."

"Who was that, sweetie?"

"Before your time."

"I should bloody well hope so."

"Anyone see that thing in the paper about Macmillan?"

"The cancer charity?"

"No, the prime minister. When he was Chancellor of the Exchequer. 'Fifty-five, 'fifty-six, something like that. A report came in making the link between smoking and cancer. Oh fuck, he thought, where's the money going to come from if we have to ban fags? Three and six in the pound extra on income tax, or whatever. Then he looked at the figures. I mean, the mortality figures. Life expectancy for a smoker: seventy-three years. Life expectancy for a nonsmoker: seventy-four."

"Is that true?"

"That's what it said. So Macmillan wrote on the report: 'Treasury think revenue interest outweighs this.'"

"It's the hypocrisy I can't stand."

"Did Macmillan smoke?"

"Pipe *and* cigarettes."

"One year. One year's difference. It's amazing when you think about it."

"Maybe we should all take it up again. Just round this table. Secret defiance of a PC world."

"Why shouldn't people smoke themselves to death? If you only lose a year."

"Not forgetting the hideous pain and suffering before you get to be the dying seventy-three-year-old."

"Reagan advertised Chesterfields, didn't he? Or was it Lucky Strike?"

"What's that got to do with it?"

"It must have *something* to do with it."

"It's the hypocrisy I can't stand."

"You keep saying that."

"Well, it is. That's why I do. Governments telling people it's bad for them while living off the tax. Cigarette companies know-ing it's bad for people and selling their stuff to the Third World because of getting sued here."

"Developing World, not Third World. We don't say that anymore."

"The Developing-Cancer World."

"Not to mention the Humphrey Bogart thing. Remember when they wanted to put him on a stamp and he was smoking in the photo so they airbrushed it out? In case people were stick-ing a stamp on a letter and saw Bogey smoking and suddenly thought: well, that looks like a good idea."

"They'll probably find a way of cutting the smoking out of films. Like colourising black-and-white movies."

"When I was growing up in South Africa, the censorship board cut any film that showed normal contact between blacks and whites. They got Island in the Sun down to about twenty-four minutes."

"Well, most films are too long."

"I didn't realise you grew up in South Africa."

"And the other thing was, everyone smoked in cinemas. Remember that? You watched the screen through a great haze of smoke."

"Ashtrays in the armrests."

"Right."

"But the thing about Bogey smoking . . . Sometimes, when I'm watching an old film, and there's a scene in a nightclub with a couple drinking and smoking and swapping bons mots, I think: this is so fucking glamorous. And then I think: actually, can I have a cigarette and a drink right now?"

"It was glamorous."

"Apart from the cancer."

"Apart from the cancer."

"And the hypocrisy."

"Well, don't inhale."

"Passive hypocrisy?"

"It happens. All the time."

"Is 'colourise' a proper verb, by the way?"

"And does anyone want coffee?"

"Only if you've got a cigarette."

"That was always part of it, wasn't it? The cigarette with the coffee."

"I don't think there are any in the house. Jim left some Gauloises when he stayed, but they're so strong we threw them away."

"And that friend of yours left some Silk Cut, but they're too weak."

"We were in Brazil last year and the health warnings out there are apocalyptic. Colour pictures on the packet of hideous things—deformed babies, pickled lungs and stuff. And the warnings . . . None of that polite 'Her Majesty's Government' stuff. Or 'The surgeon general has determined.' They tell you which bits will drop off. There was this guy who went into a shop and bought a packet of . . . I forget which brand. And he comes out, looks at the health warning, goes back in, hands the packet back and says, 'These ones make you impotent. Can I have a packet that gives me cancer?'"

"Yes."

"Well, I thought it was funny."

"Perhaps you've told them the story before, darling."

"The buggers could still laugh. It's my wine they're drinking."

"It was more the way you told it, Phil. Need to tighten the narrative."

"Bastard."

"I think we've got some grass someone left."

"Have we?"

"Yes, in the fridge door."

"Where in the fridge door?"

"The shelf with the Parmesan and the tomato paste."

"Who left it?"

"Can't remember. It must be quite old. Probably lost its jizz by now."

"Does it lose its jizz?"

"Everything loses its jizz."

"Presidential candidates?"

"Them more than anyone."

"I offered it to Doreena."

"Who's Doreena?"

"Our cleaner."

"Doreena the Cleaner. Are you having us on?"

"You offered it to *Doreena*?"

"Sure. Is it against the Employment Act or something? Anyway, she didn't want it. Said she didn't do that stuff anymore."

"Christ, what's the world coming to when one's cleaner refuses an offer of free drugs?"

"Of course, we know cigarettes are more addictive than anything. Alcohol, soft drugs, hard drugs. More addictive than heroin."

"Do we know that?"

"Well, I read it in the paper. Cigarettes top of the list."

"Then we know it."

"More addictive than power?"

"Now there's the question."

"We also know—but not from the papers—that all smokers are liars."

"So you're calling us all ex-liars?"

"Yup. And I'm one too."

"Are you going to be more specific?"

"You lie to your parents when you take it up. You lie about how many you smoke—either under or over. Oh, I'm a four-pack-a-day man, like I've got the biggest cock. Or, Oh, we only have one occasionally. That means three a day, minimum. Then you lie about it when you try to give up. And you lie to your doctor when you get cancer. Oh, I never smoked *that* much."

"Bit hard-line."

"True, though. Sue and I used to cheat on one another."

"Dav-*id*."

"I only mean about cigarettes, sweetie. 'I just had one at lunchtime.' And 'No, the others were smoking, that's what you can smell.' We both did that."

"So vote for the nonsmoker. Vote Hillary."

"Too late. Anyway, I think smokers just lie about smoking. Like drinkers just lie about drinking."

"That's not true. I've known drinkers. Serious drinkers lie about *everything*. So they can drink. And I've lied about other things so I could smoke. You know, 'I'll just go outside and get some fresh air,' or 'No, I've got to get back to the kids.'"

"OK, so we're saying, smokers and drinkers are general liars."

"Vote Hillary."

"We're saying, all liars indulge in lying."

"That's too philosophical for this time of night."

"Self-deceivers, too, that's the other thing. Our friend Jerry was a big smoker—he was of that generation. Went for a general checkup in his sixties and was told he had prostate cancer. Opted for radical surgery. They took his balls away."

"They took his balls away?"

"Yup."

"So—so he had just a cock?"

"Well, they gave him prosthetic balls."

"What are they made of?"

"I don't know—plastic, I think. Anyway, they're the same weight. So you don't notice."

"So you don't *notice*?"

"Do they make them move around like real ones?"

"Are we getting off the subject?"

"Do you know what French slang for balls is? *Les valseuses.* The waltzers. Because they move around."

"Is that female? I mean feminine. *Valseuses.*"

"Yes."

"Why is bollocks feminine in French?"

"We're definitely getting off the subject."

"*Testicules* isn't. But *valseuses* is."

"Female bollocks. Trust the French."

"No wonder they didn't support the Iraq war."

"Not that anyone around this table did."

"I was sort of sixty/forty."

"How can you be sixty/forty on something like Iraq? It's like being sixty/forty on flat-earth theory."

"I'm sixty/forty on that too."

"Anyway, the reason I brought up Jerry was because he said he was relieved when they told him he had prostate cancer. He said if it'd been lung cancer, he'd have had to give up smoking."

"So he carried on?"

"Yup."

"And?"

"Well, he was OK for a few years. Quite a few years. Then the cancer came back."

"Did he give up then?"

"No. He said there was no point giving up at that stage—he'd rather have the pleasure. I remember the last time we visited him in hospital. He was sitting up in bed watching the cricket with a huge ashtray full of butts in front of him."

"The hospital let him *smoke*?"

"It was a private room. It was a private hospital. And this was some years ago. He'd paid—it was his room. That was the attitude."

"Why were you telling us about this guy?"

"I can't remember now. You distracted me."

"Self-deception."

"That's right—self-deception."

"Sounds like the opposite to me—as if he knew exactly what he was doing. Maybe he decided it was worth it."

"That's what I mean by self-deception."

"In which case being a smoker is a necessary training for being president."

"I really think Obama can do it. As your token American."

"I agree. Well, I'm sixty/forty on it."

"You're a liberal—you're sixty/forty on everything."

"I'm not sure I'd agree."

"See, he's even sixty/forty on whether or not he's sixty/forty."

"By the way, you're wrong about Reagan."

"He didn't advertise Chesterfields?"

"No, I mean he didn't die of lung cancer."

"I didn't say he did."

"Didn't you?"

"No. He had Alzheimer's."

"Statistically, smokers get Alzheimer's much less than nonsmokers."

"That's because they're already dead by the time it normally strikes."

"New Brazilian health warning: 'These Cigarettes Help Avoid Alzheimer's.'"

"We picked up a New York Times the other week. We were on a flight. There was a report about a study of life expectancy and the comparative cost to the government, or rather the country, of different ways of dying. And those statistics Macmillan was given—when was that?"

"'Fifty-five, 'fifty-six, I think."

"Well, they're all to cock. Probably were at the time too. If you're a smoker you tend to die in your mid-seventies. If you're obese, you tend to die around eighty. And if you're a healthy, nonsmoking, nonobese person, you tend to die at an average of about eighty-four."

"They need a study to tell us that?"

"No, they need a study to tell us this: the cost in health care to the nation. And this was the thing. Smokers were the cheapest. Next came obese people. And all those healthy, nonobese, nonsmokers ended up being the biggest drain of all on the country."

"That's amazing. That's the most important thing anyone's said all evening."

"Apart from how good the lamb was."

"Stigmatising smokers, taxing the fuck out of them, making them stand on street corners in the rain, instead of thanking them for being the nation's cheap dates."

"It's the hypocrisy I can't stand."

"Anyway, smokers are nicer than nonsmokers."

"Apart from giving nonsmokers cancer."

"I don't think there's any medical basis for the theory of passive smoking."

"Nor do I. Not being a doctor. Just as you aren't."

"I think it's more a metaphor really. Like, don't invade my space."

"A metaphor for US foreign policy. Are we back to Iraq?"

"What I meant was, well, it always seemed to me that when everyone smoked, nonsmokers were nicer. Now it's the other way round."

"The persecuted minority is always nicer? Is that what Joanna's saying?"

"I'm saying there's a camaraderie. If you go up to someone on the pavement outside a pub or a restaurant and ask to buy a cigarette, they'll always give you one."

"I thought you didn't smoke."

"No, but if I did, they would."

"I spy a late switch into the conditional tense."

"I told you, all smokers are liars."

"Sounds like a matter to be discussed after we've all departed."

"What's Dick laughing at?"

"Oh, prosthetic balls. It's just the idea. Or the phrase. Multiple application, I'm sure. French foreign policy, Hillary Clinton."

"Dick."

"I'm sorry, I'm just an old-fashioned guy."

"You're just an old-fashioned child."

"Ouch. But Mummy, when I grow up, will I be allowed to smoke?"

"All this stuff about politicians needing balls. It's just . . . bollocks."

"Touché."

"You know, I'm surprised that pal of yours didn't go back to the doctor, or the surgeon, and say, Can I have a different sort of cancer instead of the one that makes you chop my bollocks off?"

"It wasn't like that. He had a choice of different approaches. He chose the most radical."

"You can say that again. Nothing sixty/forty about it."

"How can you do sixty/forty when you've only got two balls?"

"Sixty/forty is a metaphor."

"Is it?"

"Everything's a metaphor at this time of night."

"On which note, can you call us a literal taxi?"

"Do you remember the morning after a big smoke? The cigarette hangover?"

"Most mornings. The throat. The dry nose. The chest."

"And the way it was clearly separable from the booze hangover you often had at the same time."

"Booze makes you loose, fags make you tight."

"Eh?"

"Smoking constricts the blood vessels. That's why you could never start the day with a decent crap."

"Was that why?"

"Speaking as a nondoctor, that was your problem."

"So we're back where we began?"

"Which is where?"

"The inverted plastic bag and—"

"Dick, now we really *are* going."

But we didn't. We stayed, and talked some more, and decided that Obama would beat McCain, that the Conservatives were only temporarily indistinguishable from the Labour Party, that al-Qaida would certainly attack the 2012 Olympics, that in a few years Londoners would start getting nostalgic about bendy buses, that in a few decades vineyards would once again be planted along Hadrian's Wall as in Roman times, and that, in all probability, for the rest of the life of the planet, some people somewhere would always be smoking, the lucky buggers.

# Sleeping with John Updike

"I THOUGHT THAT went very well," Jane said, patting her handbag as the train doors closed with a pneumatic thump. Their carriage was nearly empty, its air warm and stale.

Alice knew to treat the remark as a question seeking reassurance. "You were certainly on good form."

"Oh, I had a nice room for a change. It always helps."

"They liked that story of yours about Graham Greene."

"They usually do," Jane replied with a slight air of complacency.

"I've always meant to ask you, is it true?"

"You know, I never worry about that anymore. It fills a slot."

When had they first met? Neither could quite remember. It must have been nearly forty years ago, during that time of interchangeable parties: the same white wine, the same hysterical noise level, the same publishers' speeches. Perhaps it had been at a PEN do, or when they'd been shortlisted for the same literary prize. Or maybe during that long, drunken summer when Alice had been sleeping with Jane's agent, for reasons she could no longer recall or, even at the time, justify.

"In a way, it's a relief we're not famous."

"Is it?" Jane looked puzzled, and a little dismayed, as if she thought they were.

"Well, I imagine we'd have readers coming to see us time and again. They'd expect some new anecdotes. I don't think either of us has told a new story in years."

"Actually, we *do* have people coming to see us again and again. Just fewer than . . . if we were famous. Anyway, I think they like hearing the same stories. When we're onstage we're not literature, we're sitcom. You have to have catchphrases."

"Like your Graham Greene story."

"I think of that as a bit more than a . . . catchphrase, Alice."

"Don't prickle, dear. It doesn't suit." Alice couldn't help noticing the sheen of sweat on her friend's face. All from the effort of getting from taxi to platform, then platform to train. And why did women carrying rather more poundage than was wise think floral prints were the answer? Bravado rarely worked with clothes, in Alice's opinion—at least, after a certain age.

When they had become friends, both were freshly married and freshly published. They had watched over each other's children, sympathised through divorces, recommended each other's books as Christmas reading. Each privately liked the other's work a little less than they said, but then, they also liked everyone else's work a little less than they said, so hypocrisy didn't come into it. Jane was embarrassed when Alice referred to herself as an artist rather than a writer, and thought her books strove to appear more highbrow than they were; Alice found Jane's work rather formless, and at times bleatingly autobiographical. Each had had a little more success than they had anticipated, but less, looking back, than they thought they deserved. Mike Nichols had taken an option on Alice's *Triple Sec*, but eventually pulled out; some journeyman from telly had come in and made it crassly sexual. Not that Alice put it like this; she would say, with a faint smile, that the adaptation had "skimped on the book's withholdingness," a phrase some found baffling. Jane, for her part, had been second favourite for the Booker with *The Primrose Path*, had spent a fortune on a frock, rehearsed her speech with Alice, and then lost out to some fashionable Antipodean.

"Who did you hear it from, just out of interest?"

"What?"

"The Graham Greene story."

"Oh, that chap . . . you know, that chap who used to publish us both."

"Jim?"

"Yes, that's right."

"Jane, how can you possibly forget Jim's name?"

"Well, I just did." The train blasted through some village halt, too fast to catch the signboard. Why did Alice need to be so stern? She wasn't exactly spotless herself. "By the way, did you ever sleep with him?"

Alice frowned slightly. "You know, to be perfectly honest, I can't remember. Did you?"

"I can't either. But I suppose if you did, then I probably did as well."

"Doesn't that make me sound a bit of a tart?"

"I don't know. I thought it made *me* sound more of a tart." Jane laughed, to cover the uncertainty.

"Do you think it's good or bad—the fact that we can't remember?"

Jane felt back onstage, facing a question she was unprepared for. So she reacted as she usually did there, and referred the matter back to Alice: the team leader, head girl, moral authority.

"What do *you* think?"

"Good, definitely."

"Why?"

"Oh, I think it's best to have a Zen approach to that sort of thing."

Sometimes, Alice's poise could make her rather too oblique

for ordinary mortals. "Are you saying it's Buddhist to forget who you slept with?"

"It could be."

"I thought Buddhism was about things coming round again in different lives?"

"Well, that would explain why we slept with so many pigs."

They looked at one another companionably. They made a good team. When they were first asked to literary festivals, they soon realised it would be more fun to appear as a double act. Together they had played Hay and Edinburgh, Charleston and King's Lynn, Dartington and Dublin; even Adelaide and Toronto. They travelled together, saving their publishers the cost of minders. Onstage, they finished one another's sentences, covered up each other's gaffes, were satirically punitive with male interviewers who tried to patronise them, and urged signing queues to buy the other one's books. The British Council had sent them abroad a few times until Jane, less than entirely sober, had made some unambassadorial remarks in Munich.

"What's the worst thing anyone's done to you?"

"Are we still talking bed?"

"Mmm."

"Jane, what a question."

"Well, we're bound to be asked it sooner or later. The way everything's going."

"I've never been raped, if that's what you're asking. At least," Alice went on reflectively, "not what the courts would call rape."

"So?"

When Alice didn't answer, Jane said, "I'll look at the landscape while you're thinking." She gazed, with vague benignity, at trees, fields, hedgerows, livestock. She had always been a town person, and her interest in the countryside was largely pragmatic, a flock of sheep only signifying roast lamb.

"It's not something . . . obvious. But I'd say it was Simon."

"Simon as in the novelist or as in the publisher or as in Simon but you don't know him?"

"Simon the novelist. It was not long after I was divorced. He phoned up and suggested coming round. Said he'd bring a bottle of wine. Which he did. When it became pretty clear that he wasn't going to get what he'd come for, he corked up the rest of it and took the bottle home."

"What was it?"

"What do you mean?"

"Well, was it champagne?"

Alice thought for a moment. "It can't have been champagne because you can't get the cork back into the bottle. Do you mean was it French or Italian or white or red?"

Jane could tell from the tone that Alice was riled. "I don't know what I meant actually. That's bad."

"What's bad? Not remembering what you meant?"

"No, putting the cork back in the bottle. Really bad." She left an ex-actress's pause. "I suppose it might have been symbolic."

Alice giggled, and Jane could tell the moment had only been a hiccup. Encouraged, she put on her sitcom voice. "Got to laugh after a bit, haven't you?"

"I suppose so," replied Alice. "It's either that or get religion."

Jane might have let the moment pass. But Alice's reference to Buddhism had given her courage, and besides, what are friends for? Even so, she looked out of the window to confess. "Actually, I've got it, if you want to know. A little, anyway."

"Really? Since when? Or rather, why?"

"A year or two. It sort of makes sense of things. Makes it all feel less . . . hopeless." Jane stroked her handbag, as if it too needed consolation.

Alice was surprised. In her worldview, everything *was* hopeless, but you just had to get on with it. And there wasn't much point changing what you believed at this late stage of the game.

She considered whether to answer seriously or lightly, and decided on the latter.

"As long as your god allows drinking and smoking and fornication."

"Oh, he's very keen on all of those."

"How about blasphemy? I always think that's the key test when it comes to a god."

"He's indifferent. He sort of rises above it."

"Then I approve."

"That's what he does. Approves."

"Makes a change. For a god, I mean. Mostly they disapprove."

"I don't think I'd want a god who disapproved. Get enough of that in life anyway. Mercy and forgiveness and understanding, that's what we need. Plus the notion of some overall plan."

"Did he find you or you find him, if that makes sense as a question?"

"Perfect sense," replied Jane. "I suppose you could say it was mutual."

"That sounds . . . comfy."

"Yes, most people don't think a god ought to be comfy."

"What's that line? Something like: 'God will forgive me, it's his job'?"

"Quite right too. I think we've overcomplicated God down the ages."

The sandwich trolley came past, and Jane ordered tea. From her handbag she took a slice of lemon in a plastic box, and a miniature of cognac from the hotel minibar. She liked to play a little unacknowledged game with her publishers: the better her room, the less she pillaged. Last night she had slept well, so contented herself with only the cognac and whisky. But once, in Cheltenham, after a poor audience and a lumpy mattress, she was in such a rage that she'd taken everything: the alcohol, the peanuts, the chocolate, the bottle opener, even the ice tray.

The trolley clattered away. Alice found herself regretting the days of proper restaurant cars with silver service and white-jacketed waiters skilled at delivering vegetables with clasped fork and spoon while outside the landscape lurched. Life, she thought, was mostly about the gradual loss of pleasure. She and Jane had given up sex at about the same time. She was no longer interested in drink; Jane had stopped caring about food—or at least, its quality. Alice gardened; Jane did crosswords, occasionally saving time by filling in answers which couldn't possibly be right.

Jane was glad Alice never rebuked her for taking a drink earlier than some. She felt a rush of affection for this poised, unmessy friend who always made sure that they caught their train.

"That was a nice young man who interviewed us," said Alice. "Properly respectful."

"He was to you. But he did that thing to me."

"What thing?"

"Didn't you notice?" Jane gave a sigh of self-pity. "When he mentioned all those books that my latest reminded him of. And you can't very well say you haven't read some of them or you'll look like an ignoramus. So you go along with it and then everyone assumes that's where you got your ideas from."

Alice thought this unduly paranoid. "They weren't thinking that, Jane. More likely they were writing him down as a show-off. And they loved it when he mentioned *Moby-Dick* and you put your head on one side and said, 'Is that the one with the whale?'"

"Yes."

"Jane, you're not telling me you haven't read *Moby-Dick*?"

"Did it look as if I hadn't?"

"No, not at all."

"Good. Well, I wasn't exactly lying. I saw the film. Gregory Peck. Was it good?"

"The film?"

"No, the book, silly."

"Since you ask, I haven't read it either."

"Alice, you're such a *friend*, you know."

"Do you read those young men everyone's going on about?"

"Which ones?"

"The ones everyone's going on about."

"No. I think they've got quite enough readers already, don't you?"

Their own sales were holding up, just about. A couple of thousand in hardback, twenty or so in paper. They still had a certain name recognition. Alice wrote a weekly column about life's uncertainties and misfortunes, though Jane thought it would be improved by more references to Alice's own life and fewer to Epictetus. Jane was still in demand when radio programmes needed someone to fill the Social Policy/Woman/Nonprofessional/Humour slot; though one producer had firmly added "BIM" to her contact details, meaning "Best in Morning."

Jane wanted to keep the mood going. "What about the young women everyone's going on about?"

"I suppose I pretend a little more to have read them than with the boys."

"So do I. Is that bad?"

"No, I think it's sisterly."

Jane flinched as a great wind blast from a train going in the opposite direction suddenly rocked them. Why on earth did they put the tracks so close together? And instantly her head was full of helicopter news footage: carriages jackknifed—they always used that verb, making it sound the more violent—trains strewn at the bottom of embankments, flashing lights, stretcher crews and, in the background, one carriage mounting another like mating metal. Quickly her mind ran on to plane crashes, mass slaughter, cancer, the strangling of old ladies who lived alone, and the probable absence of immortality. The God Who Approved of Things was powerless against such visions. She tipped the last of the cognac into her tea. She must get Alice to distract her.

"What are you thinking about?" she asked, timid as a first-timer in a book-signing queue.

"Actually, I was wondering if you'd ever been jealous of me."

"Why were you wondering that?"

"I don't know. Just one of those stray thoughts that arrive."

"Good. Because it's hardly kind."

"Isn't it?"

"Well, if I admit I've been jealous of you, that makes me a mean-spirited friend. And if I say I haven't, it sounds as if I'm so smug I can't find anything in your life or your books worthy of jealousy."

"Jane, I'm sorry. Put like that—I'm a bitch. Apologies."

"Accepted. But since you ask . . ."

"Are you sure I want to hear this now?" Strange how there were still times when she underestimated Jane.

". . . I don't know if 'jealous' is the right word. But I was envious as hell about the Mike Nichols thing—until it went away. And I was pretty furious when you slept with my husband, but that was anger not jealousy, I think."

"I suppose that was tactless of me. But he was your ex-husband by then. And back in those days everyone slept with everyone, didn't they?" Beneath such worldliness, Alice felt pressing irritation. This again? It wasn't as if they hadn't discussed it to death at the time. And afterwards. And Jane had written that bloody novel about it, claiming that "David" was just about to return to "Jill" when "Angela" intervened. What it didn't say in the novel was that it was two years, not two months, on, and by that time "David" was fucking half of west London as well as "Angela."

"It was tactless of you to tell me."

"Yes. I suppose I hoped you'd make me stop. I needed someone to make me stop. I was a mess at the time, wasn't I?" And they'd discussed that too. Why did some people forget what they needed to remember, and remember what was best forgotten?

"Are you sure that was the reason?"

Alice took a breath. She was damned if she was going to carry on apologising for the rest of her life. "No, I can't really remember what the reason was at the time. I'm just guessing. Post hoc," she added, as if that made it more authoritative, and closed the matter. But Jane wasn't so easily put off.

"I wonder if Derek did it because *he* wanted to make *me* jealous."

Now Alice was feeling properly cross. "Well, thank you for that. I thought he did it because he couldn't resist the many charms I had to offer in those days."

Jane remembered how much décolletage Alice used to show. Nowadays it was all well-cut trouser suits with a cashmere sweater and a silk scarf knotted around the tortoise neck. Back then it had been more like someone holding up a fruit bowl in your direction. Yes, men were simple beings, and Derek was simpler than most, so maybe it was all really about a cunning bra.

Not entirely changing the subject, she found herself asking, "Are you going to write your memoirs, by the way?"

Alice shook her head. "Too depressing."

"Remembering all that stuff?"

"No, not the remembering—or the making up. The publishing, the putting it out there. I can just about live with the fact that a distinctly finite number of people want to read my novels. But imagine writing your autobiography, trying to summarise all you've known and seen and felt and learnt and suffered in your fifty-odd years—"

"Fifty!"

"I only start counting at sixteen, didn't you know? Before that I wasn't sentient, let alone responsible for what I was."

Perhaps that was the secret of Alice's admirable, indefatigable poise. Every few years she drew a line under what had gone before and declined further responsibility. As with Derek. "Go on."

". . . only to find that there was no one extra out there wanting to know. Or perhaps even fewer people."

"You could put lots of sex in it. They like the idea of old . . ."

"Biddies?" Alice raised an eyebrow. "Bats?"

". . . bats like us coming clean about sex. Old men look boastful when they remember their conquests. Old women come across as brave."

"Be that as it may, you've got to have slept with someone famous." Derek could never be accused of fame. Nor could Simon the novelist, let alone one's own publisher. "Either that or you've got to have done something peculiarly disgusting."

Jane thought her friend was being disingenuous. "Isn't John Updike famous?"

"He only twinkled at me."

"*Alice!* I saw you with my own eyes perched on his knee."

Alice gave a tight smile. She could remember it all quite clearly: someone's flat in Little Venice, the usual faces, a Byrds LP playing, a background smell of dope, the famous visiting writer, her own sudden forwardness. "I perched, as you put it, on his knee. And he twinkled at me. End of story."

"But you told me . . ."

"No I didn't."

"But you let me understand . . ."

"Well, one has one's pride."

"You mean?"

"I *mean* he said he had an early start the next day. Paris, Copenhagen, wherever. Book tour. You know."

"The headache excuse."

"Precisely."

"Well," said Jane, trying to hide a sudden surge of jauntiness, "I've always believed that writers get more out of things going wrong than things going right. It's the only profession in which failure can be put to good use."

"I don't think 'failure' exactly describes my moment with John Updike."

"Of course not, darling."

"And you are, if you don't mind my saying so, coming on a little like a self-help book." Or like you sound on *Woman's Hour*, brightly telling others how to live.

"Am I?"

"The point is, even if personal failure *can* be properly transformed into art, it still leaves you where you were when you started."

"And where's that?"

"Not having slept with John Updike."

"Well, if it's any consolation, I'm jealous of him twinkling at you."

"You're a friend," Alice replied, but her tone betrayed her.

They fell silent. Some large station went by.

"Was that Swindon?" Jane asked, to make it sound as if they weren't quarrelling.

"Probably."

"Do you think we have many readers in Swindon?" Oh, come on, Alice, don't get huffy on me. Or rather, don't let's get huffy on one another.

"What do you think?"

Jane didn't know what to think. She was half in a panic. She reached for a sudden fact. "It's the largest town in England without a university."

"How do you know that?" Alice asked, trying to appear envious.

"Oh, it's just the sort of thing I know. I expect I got it from *Moby-Dick*."

They laughed contentedly, complicitly. Silence fell. After a while they passed Reading, and each gave the other credit for not pointing out the Gaol or going on about Oscar Wilde. Jane

went to the loo, or perhaps to consult the minibar in her handbag. Alice found herself wondering if it were better to take life
seriously or lightly. Or was that a false antithesis, merely a way
of feeling superior? Jane, it seemed to her, took life lightly, until
it went wrong, when she reached for serious solutions like God.
Better to take life seriously, and reach for light solutions. Satire,
for instance; or suicide. Why did people hold so fast to life, that
thing they were given without being consulted? All lives were
failures, in Alice's reading of the world, and Jane's platitude about
turning failure into art was fluffy fantasy. Anyone who understood art knew that it never achieved what its maker dreamt for
it. Art always fell short, and the artist, far from rescuing something from the disaster of life, was thereby condemned to be a
double failure.

When Jane returned, Alice was busy folding up the sections of
newspaper she would keep to read over her Sunday-night boiled
egg. It was strange how, as you aged, vanity became less a vice and
almost its opposite: a moral requirement. Their mothers would
have worn a girdle or corset, but their mothers were long dead,
and their girdles and corsets with them. Jane had always been
overweight—that was one of the things Derek had complained
about; and his habit of criticising his ex-wife either before or
shortly after he and Alice went to bed together had been another
reason for finishing with him. It wasn't sisterliness, more disapproval of a lack of class in the man. Subsequently, Jane had got
quite a bit larger, what with her drinking and a taste for things
like buns at teatime. Buns! There really were a few things women
should grow out of. Even if petty vices proved crowd-pleasing
when coyly confessed into a microphone. And as for Moby-Dick,
it had been perfectly clear to all and sundry that Jane had never
read a word of it. Still, that was the constant advantage of appear-
ing with Jane. It made her, Alice, look better: lucid, sober, well-
read, slim. How long would it be before Jane published a novel

about an overweight writer with a drink problem who finds a god to approve of her? Bitch, Alice thought to herself. You really could do with the scourge of one of those old, punitive religions. Stoical atheism is too morally neutral for you.

Guilt made her hug Jane a little longer as they neared the head of the taxi queue at Paddington.

"Are you going to the Authors of the Year party at Hatchards?"

"I was an Author of the Year last year. This year I'm a Forgotten Author."

"Now, don't get maudlin, Jane. But since you're not going, I shan't either." Alice said this firmly, while aware that she might later change her mind.

"So where are we off to next?"

"Is it Edinburgh?"

"Could be. That's your taxi."

"Bye, partner. You're the best."

"So are you."

They kissed again.

Later, over her boiled egg, Alice found her mind drifting from the cultural pages to Derek. Yes, he had been an oaf, but one with such an appetite for her that it had all seemed not worth questioning. And at the time Jane didn't appear to mind; only later did she start to become resentful. Alice wondered if this was something to do with Jane, or with the nature of time; but she failed to reach a conclusion, and went back to the newspaper.

Jane, meanwhile, in another part of London, was watching television, and picking up cheese on toast with her fingers, not caring where the crumbs fell. Her hand occasionally slipped a little on the wineglass. Some female Euro-politician on the news reminded her of Alice, and she thought about their long friendship, and how, when they were onstage together, Alice always played the senior partner, and she always acquiesced. Was this because she had a subservient nature, or because she thought it made her, Jane, come across as nicer? Unlike Alice, she never minded owning up to weaknesses. So maybe it was time to admit the gaps in her reading. She could start in Edinburgh. That was a trip to look forward to. She imagined these jaunts of theirs going on into the future until . . . what? The television screen was replaced by an image of herself dropping dead on a near-empty train coming back from somewhere. What did they do when that happened? Stop the train—at Swindon, say—and take the body off, or just prop her up in the seat as if she was asleep or drunk and continue on to London? There must be a protocol written down somewhere. But how could they give a place of death if she was on a moving train at the time? And what would Alice do, if her body was taken off? Would she loyally accompany her dead friend, or find some high-minded argument for staying on the train? It suddenly seemed very important to be reassured that Alice wouldn't abandon her. She looked across at the telephone, wondering what Alice was doing at that moment. But then she imagined the small, disapproving silence before Alice answered her question, a silence which would somehow imply that her friend was needy, self-dramatising and overweight. Jane sighed, reached for the remote, and changed the channel.

# At Phil & Joanna's 2: Marmalade

IT WAS the kind of mid-February which reminds the British why so many of their compatriots chose emigration. Snow had fallen intermittently since October, the sky was a dull aluminium, and the television news reporting flash floods, toddlers being swept away and pensioners paddled to safety. We had talked about SAD, the credit crunch, the rise in unemployment and the possibility of increased social tension.

"All I'm saying is, it's not surprising if foreign firms operating here fly in foreign labour when there are piles of job seekers at home."

"And all I'm saying is, there are more Brits working in Europe than Europeans working here."

"Did you see that Italian worker giving the finger to photographers?"

"Yes, I'm all for importing foreign labour if it looks like that."

"Don't give her any more, Phil."

"Without sounding too much like the prime minister or one of those papers we don't read, at the moment I think it should be a case of British jobs for British workers."

"And European wine for British wives."

"That's a non sequitur."

"No, it's a postprandial sequitur. Amounts to the same thing."

"As your resident alien—"

"Pray silence for the spokesman of our former colony."

". . . I recall when all you guys were arguing about joining the single currency. And I was thinking: what's their problem? I've just driven to the middle of Italy and back using a single currency and it's called MasterCard."

"If we joined the euro the pound would be worth less."

"Surely, if we joined the euro—"

"Joke."

"You've got the same colour passports. Why not cut to the chase and say you're all Europeans?"

"Because then we wouldn't be allowed to make jokes about foreigners."

"Which is after all a central British tradition."

"Look, go to any city in Europe and the stores are more or less the same. At times you wonder where you are. Internal borders hardly exist. Plastic's replacing money, the internet's replacing everything else. And more and more people speak English, which makes it even easier. So why not admit the reality?"

"But that's another British trait we cling to. Not accepting reality."

"Like hypocrisy."

"Don't get her started on that. You rode that hobbyhorse to death last time, darling."

"Did I?"

"Riding a hobbyhorse to death is flogging a dead metaphor."

"What is the difference between a metaphor and a simile, by the way?"

"Marmalade."

"Which of you two is driving?"

"Have you made yours?"

"You know, I always spot the Sevilles when they first come in and then never get around to buying any."

"One of the last fruit or veg still obedient to the concept of a season. I wish the world would go back to that."

"No you don't. You'd have turnips and swedes on the trot all winter."

"When I was a boy, we had this big sideboard in the kitchen with deep drawers at the bottom, and once a year they'd all suddenly be full of marmalade. It was like a miracle. I never saw my mum making it. I'd come home from school, and there'd be this smell, and I'd go to the sideboard, and it was all full of pots. All of them labelled. Still warm. And it had to last us the whole year."

"My dear Phil. Cue rheumy tear and violins. This was when you were stuffing newspaper into your shoes as you trudged to your holiday job at t'mill?"

"Fuck off, Dick."

"Claude says this is the last week for Sevilles."

"I knew it. I'm going to miss out again."

"There's a pun in Shakespeare on 'Seville' and 'civil.' Not that I can remember what it is."

"You can freeze them, you know."

"You should see our freezer already. I don't want it to become an even greater repository of guilt."

"Sounds like those damn bankers—repositories of gilt."

"They don't look very guilty."

"I was trying to make a pun, sweetie."

"Who's Claude?"

"He's our greengrocer. He's French. Actually, French Tunisian."

"Well, that's another thing. How many of your traditional shopkeepers are English anymore? Around here, anyway. A quarter, a third?"

"Speaking of which, did I tell you about the home bowel-screening kit the government kindly sent me now I'm officially an old git?"

"Dick, must you?"

"I promise not to offend, though the temptation is glittering."

"It's just that you get so potty-mouthed with booze."

"Then I shall be demure. Prim. Leave everything to the imagination. They send you this kit, with a plasticky envelope in which to send back the—how shall I put it?—necessary evidence. Two specimens taken on each of three separate days. And you have to fill in the date of each sample."

"How do you . . . capture the sample? Do you have to fish it out?"

"No, on the contrary. It must be uncontaminated by water."

"Then . . ."

"I have promised to restrict myself to the language of Miss Austen. I'm sure they had paper towels and little cardboard sticks back then, and probably a nursery game called Catch It If You Can."

"Dick."

"That reminds me, I had to see a proctologist once, and he told me one way to check my condition—whatever it was, I deliberately forget—was to squat down over a mirror on the floor. Somehow, I thought I'd rather risk whatever it was I might be getting."

"Doubtless some of you are wondering why I raised the subject."

"It's because you get potty-mouthed with booze."

"A sufficient but not a necessary condition. No, you see, I did my first test last Thursday, and I was just about to do the next one the next day until I realised. Friday the thirteenth. Not an auspicious day. So I did it on the Saturday instead."

"But that was—"

"Exactly. St. Valentine's Day. Love me, love my colon."

"How often do you think that happens, Friday the thirteenth followed by Valentine's Day?"

"Pass."

"Pass."

"When I was a boy—a lad—a young man—I don't think I sent a single valentine or got one. It just wasn't what . . . people I knew did. The only ones I've had have come since I've been married."

"Joanna, aren't you worried by that?"

"No. He means, I send them."

"Ah, sweet. Indeed, *schweeeet*."

"You know, I've heard of your famous English emotional reticence, but that really does set the bar high. Not sending valentines till after you're married."

"I read that there was a possible link between Seville oranges and bowel cancer."

"Did you really?"

"No, but it's the sort of thing you say when it gets late."

"You're funnier when you don't strain so much."

"I remember one of the first times I went into a lavatory stall and read the graffiti, there was one that said, 'Do not bite the knob while straining.' It took me about five years to work it out."

"Is that knob as in knob?"

"No, it's knob as in doorknob."

"Changing the subject entirely, I was in a stall once and taking my leisure when I noticed something written down at the bottom of the side wall at a sort of slant. So I bent over until I could read it, and it said, 'You are now crapping at an angle of forty-five degrees.'"

"I would just like to say that the reason I mentioned marmalade . . ."

"Apart from its link to bowel cancer."

"Is because it's such a British phenomenon. Larry was saying how we're now all the same. So instead of saying the Royal Family or whatever, I said marmalade."

"We have it in the States."

"You *have* it, in little pots in hotels at breakfast. But you don't make it in your *homes*, you don't *understand* it."

"The French have it. *Confiture d'orange.*"

"Same thing applies. That's just jam. Orange jam."

"No, it's French to begin with, it comes from '*Marie malade.*' That queen of Scotland who had French connections."

"FCUK. They were here already?"

"And Mary, Queen of Scots, or Bloody Mary, or whoever it was, was ill. And they made it for her. So *Marie malade*—marmalade. See?"

"I think we were there already."

"Anyway, I'll tell you why we Brits will always remain British."

"Don't you hate the way everyone says 'the UK' or just 'UK' nowadays? Not to mention 'UK plc' and all that."

"I think Tony Blair started it."

"I thought you blamed everything on Mrs. Thatcher."

"No, I've switched. It's all Blair's fault now."

"UK plc's just honest. We're a trading nation, always were. Thatch just reconnected us to the real England that is forever England—money worshipping, self-interested, xenophobic, culture hating. It's our default setting."

"As I was saying, do you know what we also celebrate on February the fourteenth, apart from St. Valentine's Day?"

"National Bowel-Screening Day?"

"Shut up, Dick."

"No. It's also National Impotence Day."

"I lurv your Breedish sense of yumor."

"I lurv your Croatian accent."

"But it's true. And if anyone asks me about national characteristics, or irony, for that matter, that's what I tell them: February the fourteenth."

"Blood oranges."

"Let me guess. Named after Bloody Mary."

"Did you notice a few years ago they started calling blood oranges 'ruby oranges' in supermarkets? Just in case anyone thought they might really contain blood."

"As opposed to containing rubies."

"Exactly."

"Anyway, they're just about coming into the shops, so they're overlapping with Sevilles, and I was wondering if that happens as often, say, as Friday the thirteenth precedes Valentine's Day."

"Joanna, that's another reason I love you. You're able to impose narrative coherence on the likes of us at this time of night. What could be more flattering than a hostess who can make her guests imagine they're sticking to the point?"

"Put that on next year's valentine, Phil."

"And does everyone agree tonight's blood or ruby orange salad was fit to set before a queen?"

"And the neck-of-lamb stew fit to be set before a king."

"Charles the First's final request."

"He wore two shirts."

"Charles the First?"

"On the day he was beheaded. It was extremely cold, and he didn't want to start shivering and have Ye People believe he was frightened."

"*That's* pretty British."

"All those people who dress up in period costume and fight Civil War battles all over again. That's very British too, I always think."

"Well, we do it in the States. I guess in lots of other countries too."

"OK, but we did it first. We invented it."

"Like your cricket and your soccer and your Devonshire cream teas."

"If we can stick to marmalade for the moment."

"It gives a good glaze to a duck."

"I bet everyone here who makes it does it differently and wants a different consistency."

"Runny."

"Sticky."

"Sue boils it so hard it falls off the toast if you aren't careful. No stick at all."

"Well, if you leave it too runny it pours off the toast."

"You have to put the pips in a muslin bag to get extra . . . whatsit."

"Pectin."

"That's the stuff."

"Fine cut."

"Coarse."

"I cut mine up in the Magimix."

"Cheat."

"My friend Hazel does hers in the pressure cooker."

"But that's my point. It's like boiling an egg. Or was it frying? They did a survey and discovered everyone does it differently and everyone thinks theirs is the right way."

"Is this leading anywhere, O keeper of the communal narrative?"

"What Larry was saying. About us all being the same. But we aren't. Not even with the simplest things."

"The marmalade theory of Britishness."

"That's why you shouldn't be afraid of being Europeans. All of you guys."

"I don't know if Larry was in the country when our distinguished chancellor of the exchequer, now soon-to-be-ex-prime minister, Mr. Brown, laid down a number of conditions before we would submerge the good old British pound in the filthy foreign euro."

"Converge. Not submerge. The tests for convergence."

"Can anyone remember them, by the way? Even one of them?"

"Of course not. They weren't designed to be comprehensible. They were designed to be incomprehensible, and, therefore, unmemorable."

"Why?"

"Because the decision to join the euro was always going to be political, not economic."

"That's very lucid and may even be correct."

"But does anyone think the French are less French, or the Italians less Italian, because they joined the euro?"

"The French will always be French."

"That's what they say about you."

"That we'll always be French?"

"Anyway, you don't need Seville oranges to make marmalade."

"I'm glad we're back on the subject."

"Dick's made it with every kind of citrus fruit."

"There goes my reputation."

"There was one year he made it with a mixture of—what was it?—Sevilles, sweet oranges, pink grapefruit, yellow grapefruit, lemons and limes. Six-fruit marmalade, I put on the labels."

"That wouldn't get past EU regulations."

"Remind me—mint tea, mint tea, nothing, decaf, mint tea?"

"I'll switch to nothing tonight."

"So much for my chances later on."

"David, sweetie . . ."

"Yes, Sue, sweetie?"

"OK, since you raised it. Just to ask a non-British question, have any of us, in recent memory, left Phil and Joanna's table and gone home and . . ."

"'Had a spot of old-fashioned nookie' is what she's trying to say."

"What counts as old-fashioned?"

"Oh, anything involving intromission."

"Isn't that a horrible word?"

"I was told a story about Lady Diana Cooper. Or was it Nancy Mitford? One or the other, anyway, posh. And they were—she was—on a transatlantic liner and whichever of them it was fucked one of the stewards one evening. And the next morning he ran into her in the fo'c'sle or whatever and said hello in a friendly way—"

"As one would."

"As one would. And she replied, 'Intromission is not introduction.'"

"Ah, doncha love our upper classes? There'll always be an England."

"That sort of story makes me want to stand on the table and sing 'The Red Flag.'"

"'The Ruby Flag.'"

"You're all avoiding my question."

"How can we be if we can't remember it?"

"Then shame on you."

"It's not really the alcohol, or the lack of caffeine, it's not even the tiredness. It's more that by the time we get home we're what we in our house call TFTF."

"An acronym you are about to deconstruct."

"Too Fat To Fuck."

"Talk about secrets of the bedchamber."

"You remember Jerry?"

"The guy with the plastic *testicules*?"

"I thought you'd remember that detail. Well, Jerry was abroad for a few months, and Kate—his wife—started getting worried that her tummy was a bit on the fat side. And she wanted to be in perfect shape for Jerry's return, so she went to a plastic surgeon and asked about liposuction. And the guy said yes, he could give her a flattie again . . ."

"A flattie?"

"I paraphrase the medispeak. The only downside, he said, was that she wouldn't, as he so tactfully put it, be able to take any weight on her stomach for quite a number of weeks."

"Oh-oh. Posterior intromission only."

"Don't you think, actually, that's a story about true love?"

"Unless it's a story about female insecurity."

"Hands up, all those who might like to know the derivation of the word 'marmalade.'"

"I thought you'd been a long time having a pee."

"It's nothing to do with *Marie malade*. It comes from some Greek word meaning a kind of apple grafted onto a quince."

"All the great etymologies are wrong."

"You mean, you've got another example?"

"Well, *posh*."

"Port out, starboard home, best accommodation to and from India, quarters on the side sheltered from the sun. Word applied to Lady Diana Cooper and Nancy Mitford."

"Afraid not. 'Origin unknown.'"

"That's not a derivation, 'origin unknown.'"

"It says, 'Possibly connected to a Romany word for money.'"

"That's most unsatisfactory."

"Sorry to be a spoilsport."

"Do you think that's another national characteristic?"

"Being a spoilsport?"

"No. Inventing fanciful derivations and acronyms."

"Perhaps UK really stands for something else."

"Uro Konvergence."

"It's not that late, is it?"

"Maybe it doesn't stand for anything at all."

"It's an allegory."

"Or a metaphor."

"Will someone *please* explain the difference between a simile and a metaphor?"

"A simile's . . . more similar. A metaphor's more . . . metaphorical."

"Thanks."

"It's a question of convergence, as the prime minister put it. At the moment, the euro and the pound are miles apart, so their relationship is metaphorical. Maybe even metaphysical. Then they become close, like similes, and there's convergence."

"And we finally become Europeans."

"And live happily ever after."

"Teaching them all about marmalade."

"Why didn't you guys join the euro, as a matter of fact?"

"We had the introduction, we just didn't want the intromission."

"We were too fat to fuck at the time."

"Too fat to *be* fucked. By some lean and hungry Eurocrat."

"I think we should join on St. Valentine's Day."

"Why not Friday the thirteenth?"

"No, it has to be the fourteenth. The celebration of both love and impotence. *That*'s the day we become fully paid-up members of Europe."

"Larry, do you want to know how this country's changed in my lifetime? When I was growing up, we didn't think about ourselves as a nation. There were certain assumptions, of course, but it was a sign, a proof, of who we were that we didn't think much about who or what we were. What we was was normal—or is it 'what we were was normal'? Now, this might have been due to the long overhang of imperial power, or it might be a matter of what you earlier called our emotional reticence. We weren't self-conscious. Now we are. No, we're worse—worse than self-conscious, worse than navel-gazing. Who was saying about that proctologist who told him to squat over a mirror? That's what we're like now—arse-gazing."

"Mint tea, another mint tea here, that's the decaf. I've ordered two minicabs. Why the silence? Did I miss something?"

"Only a simile."

After that, we talked about holidays, and who was going where, and how the days were getting longer, apparently at the rate of one minute per day, a fact which no one disputed, and then someone described looking at the inside of a snowdrop, and how you lifted the head of the flower expecting it to be all white inside as well, only to discover a lacy pattern of the purest green. And how different varieties of snowdrop had different internal patterns, some almost geometrical, others quite extravagant, although it was always the same green, and of a vibrancy that made you feel spring was eager to arrive. But before anyone could say anything about or against that, there was a concerted and impatient hooting from the street.

# Gardeners' World

THEY HAD REACHED the stage, eight years into their relationship, when they had started giving each other useful presents, ones that confirmed their joint project in life rather than expressed their feelings. As they unwrapped sets of coat hangers, storage jars, an olive stoner or an electric pencil sharpener, they would say, "Just what I needed," and mean it. Even gifts of underwear nowadays seemed more practical than erotic. One wedding anniversary, he'd given her a card that read, "I have cleaned all your shoes"—and he had, spraying everything suede against the rain, dabbing whitener on an old pair of tennis pumps she still wore, giving her boots a military shine, and treating the rest of her footwear with polish, brush, rag, cloth, elbow grease, devotion, love.

Ken had offered to waive presents this year, as his birthday fell only six weeks after they moved into the house, but she declined to be let off. So, this Saturday lunchtime, he gently palpated the two parcels in front of him, trying to imagine what they might contain. He used to do this out loud, but if he guessed right she was visibly disappointed, and if he guessed silly, disappointed in a different way. So now he addressed only himself. First one, soft: got to be something to wear.

"Gardening gloves! Just what I needed." He tried them on,

admired their mixture of flexibility and robustness, commented on the leather bands which reinforced the stripy canvas at key points. This was the first time they had owned a garden, and his first pair of such gloves.

His other present was some kind of oblong box; when he was about to give it a shake, she warned that some bits were fragile. He unpeeled the Sellotape carefully, as they saved wrapping paper for reuse. Inside he found a green plastic attaché case. Frowning, he raised its lid and saw a line of glass test tubes with corks in the top, a set of plastic bottles containing different coloured liquids, a long plastic spoon, and assorted mysterious dibbers and wodgers. Had he been guessing silly, he might have suggested an advanced version of the home pregnancy kit they had once used way back, when they were still hoping. Now he knew not to mention the comparison. Instead, he read the title of the handbook.

"A soil-testing kit! Just what I needed."

"They really work, apparently."

It was a good present, appealing to—what, exactly?—perhaps that small area of masculinity which modern society's erosion of difference between the sexes had not yet eliminated. Man as boffin, as prospective hunter-gatherer, as Boy Scout: a bit of each. Among their circle of friends, both sexes shared the shopping, cooking, housework, child care, driving, earning. Apart from putting on their own clothes, there was almost nothing one partner did that the other was not equally capable of. And equally willing, or unwilling, to do. But a soil-testing kit, now that was definitely a boy thing. Clever Martha does it again.

The handbook said the kit would test for potassium, phosphorus, potash and pH, whatever that was. And then presumably you got bags of different stuff and dug them in. He smiled at Martha.

"So I suppose it will also help us work out what will grow best where."

When she only smiled back, he assumed that she assumed he

was referring to the contentious subject of his vegetable patch. His theoretical vegetable patch. The one which she said there was no room for, and anyway no need for, given the farmers' market every Saturday morning in the nearby school playground. Not to mention the lead content likely to occur in any vegetables grown so close to one of the chief arterial roads leading out of London. He had pointed out that most cars nowadays used lead-free petrol.

"Well then, diesel," she had replied.

He didn't—still—see why he shouldn't have a little square patch down by the end wall, which already had a blackberry on it. He could grow potatoes and carrots, perhaps. Or Brussels sprouts, which, he had once read, sweeten up as soon as the first hard frost hits them. Or broad beans. Or anything. Even salad. He could grow lettuces and herbs. He could have a compost heap and they could do even more recycling than they did already.

But Martha was against it. Almost as soon as they had made an offer on the house she started clipping and filing articles by various horticultural sages. Many were on the subject of How to Make the Most of a Tricky Space; and no one could deny that what owners of terrace houses like theirs ended up with—a long thin strip bounded by yellow-grey brick walls—was indeed a Tricky Space. The classier gardening writers tended to suggest that in order to Make the Most of It, you should break it up into a series of small, intimate areas with different plantings and different functions, perhaps linked by a serpentine path. Before and After photos demonstrated the transformation. A nook designed to catch the sun would give way to a little rose garden, a water feature, a place where plants were grown just for the colour of their leaves, a hedged square containing a sundial, and so on. Sometimes Japanese principles were invoked. Ken, who like most of the inhabitants of the street considered himself tolerant and open-minded in matters of race, told Martha that while the Japanese had many admirable qualities, he didn't know why they should create a Japanesey garden any more than she should wear a kimono. Privately, he thought the whole notion poncey. Terrace for sitting out, preferably with barbecue area, plus grass, borders, veg patch—that was his idea of a garden.

"Don't you think I'd look good in a kimono?" she had asked, turning the argument.

Anyway, she assured him, he was taking things far too literally. They weren't going to have flowering cherries and koi carp and gongs; it was more a sensible way of interpreting a general principle. Besides, he liked the way she did salmon steaks with a soy-sauce marinade, didn't he?

"I bet the Japanese grow vegetables," he had replied, mock-grumpily.

Martha's interest in gardening had come as a surprise to him. When they had first met, she owned a window box in which she grew a few herbs; later, when they moved in together, they acquired access to a shared roof terrace. Here she kept a few terracotta planters with chives, mint, thyme and rosemary, some of which, they suspected, were stolen by their neighbours; also the bay tree her sentimentally interfering parents had given them as an augury of marital good fortune. It had been repotted a couple of times, and now stood immoveably outside their front door in a thick wooden tub.

Marriage was a democracy of two, he liked to say. He had somehow assumed that the garden would be decided upon much as the house had been, by a process of reasoned yet enthusiastic consultation in which requirements were enunciated, mutual tastes considered, finances estimated. As a consequence, there was almost nothing he actively hated in the house, and much he approved of. Now he found himself silently resenting the catalogues of teakware that arrived, the horticultural magazines piled on Martha's bedside table, and her habit of shushing him when

*Gardeners' Question Time* was on the radio. He would eavesdrop on matters of leaf curl and black spot, some new threat to wisteria, and advice about what to plant beneath an elder tree on a north-facing slope. He didn't feel threatened by Martha's new interest, just found it excessive.

pH, he learnt, was a number used to express degrees of acidity or alkalinity in solutions, formerly the logarithm to base 10 of the reciprocal of the concentration of hydrogen ions, but now related by formula to a standard solution of potassium hydrogen phthalate, which has value 4 at 15 degrees centigrade. Well, sod that for a game of soldiers, Ken thought. Why not just get a bag of bonemeal and a sack of compost and dig them in? But Ken was aware of this trait of his, a tendency to settle for the approximate, which one irate girlfriend called "just being incredibly fucking *lazy*"—a description he had always cherished.

And so he read most of the instructions that came with his soil-testing kit, identified several key locations in the garden, and proudly pulled on his new gloves before digging small samples of earth and crumbling them into the test tubes. As he added drops of liquid, inserted the corks, and shook the contents up and down, he occasionally glanced towards the kitchen window, hoping that Martha would be tenderly amused by his professionalism. His attempt at professionalism, anyway. He left each experiment the required number of minutes, took out a little notebook and recorded his findings; then he went on to the next location. Once or twice he retested when the first result had been dubious or unclear.

Martha could tell he was in a jolly mood that evening. He stirred the fricassee of rabbit, decided to give it another twenty minutes or so, poured them each a glass of white wine, and sat on the arm of her chair. Looking down indulgently at an article about different types of gravel, he played with the hair at the nape of her neck, and said, with a cheery smile,

"Bad news, I'm afraid."

She looked up, uncertain where his remark might fall on a scale from gentle tease to full critical objection.

"I've tested the soil. In places I had to do it more than once before I was confident of my findings. But the surveyor-general is now ready to report."

"Yes?"

"According to my analysis, madam, there is no soil in your soil."

"I don't understand."

"It is impossible to address deficiencies in the terroir, because there is no soil in your soil."

"You've said that. So what is there instead?"

"Oh, stones mainly. Dust, roots, clay, ground elder, dogshit, catcrap, bird droppings, stuff like that."

He liked the way he had said "your soil."

On another Saturday morning three months later, with the December sun so low that the garden would be lucky to get the slightest warmth or light, Ken came into the house and threw down his gardening gloves.

"What have you done with the blackberry?"

"What blackberry?"

This made him more tense. Their garden was hardly that big.

"The one along the back wall."

"Oh, that briar."

"That briar was a blackberry with blackberries on it. I brought you two and personally fed them into your mouth."

"I'm planning something along that wall. Maybe a Russian vine, but that's a bit cowardly. I was thinking a clematis."

"You dug up my blackberry."

"Your blackberry?" She was always at her coolest when she

knew, and knew that he knew, that she'd done something with-out consultation. Marriage was a democracy of two, except when there's a tied vote, in which case it descends into autocracy. "It was a god-awful briar."

"I had plans for it. I was going to improve its pH factor. Prune it, and stuff. Anyway, you knew it was a blackberry. Blackber-ries," he added authoritatively, "produce blackberries."

"OK, it was a bramble."

"A bramble!" This was getting ridiculous. "Brambles produce bramble jelly, which is made from blackberries."

"Do you think you could check what we need to dig into the soil to help a clematis on a north-facing wall?"

Yes, he thought, I might very well leave you. But until then, forget it, change the subject.

"It's going to be a hard winter. The bookies are only offering six to four against a white Christmas."

"Then we must get some of that plastic fleece to protect what's vulnerable. Perhaps some straw as well."

"I'll pop along to the nearest stables." Now, suddenly, he wasn't cross anymore. If she got greater pleasure out of the gar-den, let her have it.

"I hope there's lots of snow," he said boyishly.

"Is that what we want?"

"Yup. Proper gardeners pray for a hard winter. Kills all the bugs."

She nodded, allowing him that. The two of them had come at the garden from different directions. Ken had grown up in the country, and all through his adolescence couldn't wait to get to London, to university, work, life. Nature for him represented either hostility or tedium. He remembered trying to read a book in the garden, and how the combination of shifting sun, wind, bees, ants, flies, ladybirds, birdsong and his mother's chivvy-ing made plein-air studying a nightmare. He remembered being bribed to supply his reluctant manual labour. He remembered his father's vastly overcropping vegetable beds and fruit cages. His mother would dutifully fill the chest freezer with the super-abundance of beans and peas, strawberries and currants; and then, each year, guiltily, while Dad was out, throw away any bags found to be more than two years old. Her kitchen version of crop rotation, he supposed.

Martha was a town girl, who thought nature essentially benevolent, who wondered at the miracle of germination, and badgered him to go on country walks. She had developed an autodidact's zeal in recent months. He thought of himself as an instinctive amateur, her as a technocrat.

"More bookwork?" he asked mildly, as he got into bed. She was reading Ursula Buchan's *Wall Plants and Climbers*.

"There's nothing wrong with bookwork, Ken."

"As I know to my cost," he replied, turning out his bedside light.

This wasn't an argument, not anymore; just an admitted difference. Martha, for instance, thought that it was only sensible to follow recipes when cooking. "Can't make an omelette without breaking the spine of a cookbook?"—as he had once, ponderously, put it. Whereas he preferred just to glance at a recipe to give himself ideas, and then wing it. She liked guidebooks, and used a map even when walking through town; he preferred an internal compass, serendipity, the joy of getting creatively lost. This led to various quarrels in the car.

She had also pointed out to him that, when it came to sex, their positions were reversed. He had confessed to a lot of preliminary bookwork, whereas she, as she once expressed it, had learnt on the job. He'd replied that he hoped he wasn't meant to take that literally. Not that there was anything wrong with their sex life—in his opinion, anyway. Perhaps they had what was needed in any partnership: one bookworm and one instinctivist.

As he thought about this, he found himself with what felt to him like a monster erection, which seemed to have crept up unawares. He turned on his side towards Martha, and put his left hand on her hip in a way that could be interpreted as a signal or not, depending on mood.

Aware that he was awake, Martha murmured, "I was wondering about a trachelospermum jasminoides, but suspect the soil's too acid."

"Fair enough," he murmured back.

It snowed in mid-December, first a misleading light softness that turned to water as it hit the pavement, then a solid couple of inches. When Ken got home from work a thick layer of white was holding on the flat leaves of the bay tree, an incongruous sight. The next morning, he took his camera to the front door.

"The *bastards*!" he shouted back into the house. Martha came down the hall in her dressing gown. "Look, the bastards," he repeated.

Outside there was only an oak tub half-full of earth.

"I've heard about the rustling of Christmas trees . . ."

"The neighbours did warn us," she replied.

"Did they?"

"Yes, number forty-seven told us we should chain it to the wall. You said you didn't like the idea of chained trees any more than chained bears or chained slaves."

"Did I say that?"

"Yes."

"Sounds a bit pompous to me."

She put a towelling forearm through his, and they went inside again.

"Shall we call the police?"

"I expect it's already heeled in somewhere in darkest Essex," he replied.

"It's not bad luck, is it?"

"No, it's not bad luck," he said firmly. "We don't believe in bad luck. It was just some wide boy who saw it with snow on the leaves and was struck by a rare moment of aesthetic bliss."

"You're in a very indulgent mood."

"Must be Christmas or something. By the way, you know that water feature you're planning between the rose grove and the leaf display?"

"Yes." She did not respond to his caricatural terminology.

"What about mosquitoes?"

"We keep the water circulating. That way you don't get them."

"How?"

"Electric pump. We can run a cable from the kitchen."

"In that case, I have only one more objection. Can we please, please, not call it a water *feature*? Waterfall, cascade, lily pond, miniature stream, anything but *feature*."

"Ruskin said he always worked better to the sound of running water."

"Didn't it make him want to pee all the time?"

"Why should it?"

"Because it does with blokes. You might have to install a toilet feature next to it."

"You *are* in a sunny mood."

Probably it was the snow, which always cheered him. But it was also that he had secretly applied for an allotment, down between the water-purifying plant and the railway line. Someone had told him the waiting list wasn't too long.

Two days later, setting off for work, he shut the front door and stepped straight into a pile of earth.

"The *bastards!*" This time he said it to the entire street.

They had come back and taken the oak tub, leaving him the soil.

Spring was marked by a series of Saturday-morning visits to the local garden centre. Ken would drop Martha at the main entrance, then drive to the car park and spend longer than necessary lowering the backseat to make room for whatever compost, loam, peat, wood chips or gravel had been indicated by his wife's latest reading. Then he might sit in the car awhile longer, arguing that he wasn't much help in choosing anyway. He was quite happy to pay for the loaded contents of the yellow plastic wagon that usually accompanied Martha to the cash desk. In fact, that seemed to him the perfect deal: he drove her there, sat in the car, met her at the desk and paid, then drove them home and paid again by risking a hernia lifting all the stuff out of the car and lugging it through the house to the garden.

Doubtless it was something to do with his childhood, with toxic memories of trudging round nurseries while his parents chose bedding plants. Not that Ken believed in blaming his parents at this late stage: if they'd been gourmets and wine bores, he might have ended up a teetotal vegan, but still would have taken the responsibility for that condition. Even so, there was something about a garden centre—this purveyor of *rus in urbe*, with its tubs and planters and trellises, its seed packets and sproutlets and shrubs, its balls of twine and wire ties wrapped in green plastic, its slug pellets and fox-discouraging machines and watering systems and garden candles, all those verdant aisles full of hope and promise, along which processed friendly people with peeling skin and sandals waving red plastic bottles of tomato fertiliser at one another—something about all this that really got on his tits.

And it always took him back to his late adolescence, a time when for him fear and distrust of the world were about to turn into a hesitant love of it, when life was poised to lurch irretrievably in one direction or another, when, as it now seemed to him, you had a last chance to see clearly before being flung into the full business of being yourself among others, at which point things proceeded too fast for proper examination. But then, just back exactly then, he had specialised in seeing through the hypocrisy and deceit of adult life. True, his Northamptonshire village contained no obvious Rasputin or Himmler; so the great moral fault lines of humanity had to be mapped from the possibly unrepresentative sample of his parents' friends. But this made his findings the more valuable. And it had pleased him to detect vice hidden in the seemingly innocuous, not to say beneficial, occupation of gardening. Envy, greed, resentment, the costive withholding of praise and its false overlavishing, anger, lust, covetousness and various other of the deadly sins he couldn't quite remember. Murder? Well, why not? Doubtless some Dutchman had exterminated some other Dutchman to get his hands on a priceless corm or tuber or whatever they were called—yes, bulb—during the madness known as Tulipomania.

And on a more normal, decently English scale of evil, he had noticed how even old friends of his parents became tight-lipped and mean-spirited during a tour of the garden, with many a "How did you get this to flower so early?" and "Where did you track that down?" and "You're so lucky with your soil." He recalled one stout old bat in tweed jodhpurs who spent forty minutes on an early-morning examination of his parents' half acre, returning to issue only the prim bulletin of "You evidently had the frost rather earlier than we did." He'd read about otherwise virtuous citizens who travelled to the great gardens of England with concealed secateurs, and poacher's pockets in which to stow their loot. No wonder there were now security cameras and uniformed guards at some of the country's most sylvan and pastoral locations. Plant-napping was rife, and perhaps the speed with which he'd recovered from the theft of their bay tree hadn't been anything to do with the cheery snow and the season, but because it confirmed one of the key moral discoveries of his adolescence.

The previous evening they'd been sitting out on the recently delivered teak bench with a bottle of rosé between them. For once there was no inane music from a neighbour's house, no wailing car alarm, no flight-path thunder; just a silence disturbed instead by some bloody noisy birds. Ken didn't really keep up with birds, but he knew there'd been some major species shifts: far fewer sparrows and starlings than before—not that he missed either of them; the same for swallows and stuff like that; the opposite for magpies. He didn't know what it meant, or what was the cause. Pollution, slug pellets, global warming? Maybe that sly old thing called evolution. There'd also been an increase in parrots—unless they were parakeets—in many of London's parks. Some breeding pair had escaped and multiplied, managing to survive the mild English winters. Now they were screaming from the tops of plane trees; he'd even noticed one clamped to a neighbour's bird feeder.

"Why are those birds so bloody noisy?" he asked in a ruminative, fake-complaining way.

"They're blackbirds."

"Is that an answer to my question?"

"Yes," she replied.

"Care to explain to a mere country lad? Why they *need* to be so bloody loud?"

"It's territorial."

"Can't you be territorial without being noisy?"

"Not if you're a blackbird."

"Hmm."

Still, he supposed, humans were territorial too, and had tools and machinery to make the noises for them. He'd repointed the brickwork where the mortar had crumbled away, and put up trellises which heightened the party walls. He'd fixed rustic, woven-wood partitions between the various sections of the garden. He'd even paid someone to lay a winding flagged path and run an electric cable to the place where, at the turn of a switch, water would gush over large oval stones imported from some distant Scottish beach.

Also that spring he improved the soil as and where indicated. He dug where Martha asked him to dig. He began what promised to be a long campaign against ground elder. He wondered if he loved Martha just as much as ever, or if he was merely performing a husbandly routine from which others were invited to deduce how much he loved her. He was informed that he was third in the queue for an allotment. He did vocal imitations of the experts on *Gardeners' Question Time* until Martha told him it really wasn't funny anymore.

He was disturbed by a knocking close to his ear. He opened his eyes. Martha had wheeled her yellow plastic wagon, stacked to the gunnels, down to the car park.

"I even tried you on your mobile . . ."

"Sorry, love. Didn't bring it. Miles away. Have you paid?"

Martha merely nodded. She wasn't exactly cross. She half expected his head to go AWOL as soon as they drew into a garden centre. Ken got out of the car and eagerly took over loading the boot. Nothing too herniating this time, anyway, he thought.


Martha considered barbecues a bit vulgar. She didn't use the word, but didn't need to. Ken liked nothing more than the smell of meat cooking over whitened coals. She liked neither the event nor the equipment. He had suggested getting one of those small numbers—what were they called?—yes, hibachis, and actually, weren't they Japanese inventions, and therefore appropriate to this little plot of God's earth? Martha was faintly amused by yet another of his Japanese jokes, but unpersuaded. Eventually she allowed the acquisition of a sleek little terra-cotta item shaped like a miniature barrel standing on end; it was some kind of ethnic oven on special offer from the *Guardian*. Ken had to promise never to use barbecue lighter fuel with it.

Now that summer had come, they were repaying hospitality received when the house had been in chaos. The sky was still light at eight when Marion and Alex and Nick and Anne arrived, but the day's heat, never extreme to begin with, was already beginning to disappear. The two women guests immediately wished they'd worn tights and not overdone the summery look, thinking it unhostly of Martha to have knowingly dressed against the evening's chill. But since they'd been invited to eat outside, eat outside was what they would do. There were jokes about mulled wine and the Blitz spirit, and Alex pretended to warm his hands on the terra-cotta oven, nearly knocking it over in the process.

While Ken fiddled with the chicken thighs, jabbing with a skewer to see if the juices ran clear, Martha gave their guests "the tour." Since they were never more than a few yards away, Ken heard all the compliments to Martha's ingenuity. Briefly, he found himself a disaffected teenager again, trying to assess the sincerity or hypocrisy of each speaker. Then his trellises were admired—praise he took as coming entirely from the heart. The next moment, he heard Martha explaining that the far end of the garden had been "just a mass of hideous brambles when we got here."

The light was beginning to fade by the time they crouched over their pear, walnut and gorgonzola starter. Alex, who clearly hadn't been paying attention during the tour, said, "Have you left a tap on somewhere?"

Ken looked at Martha but declined to take advantage. "It's probably next door," he said. "Rather a shambolic household."

Martha looked grateful, so Ken thought it would be OK to tell his story about the soil-testing kit. He spun it out rather, elaborating his self-portrayal as mad chemist, and holding off the punch line as long as possible.

"And then I came in and said to Martha, 'Bad news, I'm afraid. There's no soil in your soil.'"

There was a gratifying laugh. And Martha joined in; she knew that from now on this was going to be one of his stories.

Feeling himself in credit, Ken decided to light the garden candles, yard-high towers of wax which blazed away and made him think vaguely of Roman triumphs. He also took the opportunity to turn off what he would always, in his own mind, refer to as the water feature.

It was now on the colder side of chilly. Ken poured more red wine, and Martha offered a move indoors, which everyone politely refused.

"Where's all this global warming when you need it?" asked Alex cheerily.

Then they talked about patio heaters—which really gave out a blast but were so unecological that it was antisocial to buy one—and carbon footprints, and the sustainability of fish stocks, and farmers' markets, and electric cars versus biodiesel, and wind farms and solar heating. Ken heard a mosquito fizz warningly at his ear; he ignored it, and didn't even wince when he felt it bite. He sat there and enjoyed being proved right.

"I've got an allotment," he announced. The marital coward's ploy of breaking news in front of friends. But Martha didn't indicate either surprise or disappointment, merely joined in the raising of glasses to Ken's laudable new hobby. He was asked about its cost and location, the condition of its soil, and what he intended to grow there.

"Blackberries," said Martha before he could answer. She was smiling at him tenderly.

"How did you guess?"

"When I was sending off the Marshalls catalogue." She had asked him to confirm her arithmetic; not that she wasn't competent to add up, but there were a lot of small sums often ending in 99p, and anyway, this was the sort of thing Ken did in their marriage. Like write the cheque too, which he had done after making a couple of additions to the order. Then he'd taken it back to Martha, because she was the Keeper of the Stamps in their marriage. "And I noticed you'd ordered two blackberry bushes. A variety called Loch Tay, I seem to remember."

"You're a terror for names," he said, looking across at her. "A terror and a whiz."

There was a short silence, as if something intimate had been mistakenly disclosed.

"You know what we could plant on the allotment," Martha began.

"What's this *we* shit, Paleface?" he responded before she could continue. It was one of their marital jokes, always had been; but one apparently unfamiliar to these particular friends, who couldn't tell if this was a vestigial quarrel. Nor could he, for that matter; he often couldn't nowadays.

As the silence continued, Marion said into it, "I don't like to mention this, but the bugs are biting." She had one hand down by her ankle.

"Our friends don't like our garden!" Ken shouted, in a voice intended to assure everyone that no quarrel was likely. But there was something hysterical in his tone, a signal for their guests to make sly marital eye contact, decline a range of teas and coffees, and prepare their final compliments.

Later, from the bathroom, he called, "Have we got some of that Hc45 stuff?"

"Have you been bitten?"

He pointed to the side of his neck.

"Christ, Ken, there are five of them. Didn't you feel it?"

"Yes, but I wasn't going to say. I didn't want anyone criticising your garden."

"Poor thing. Martyr. They must bite you because you've got sweet flesh. They leave me alone."

In bed, too tired for reading or sex, they idly summarised the evening, each encouraging the other to the conclusion that it had been a success.

"Oh bugger," he said. "I think I left a piece of chicken in the barrel thingy. Maybe I'd better go down and bring it in."

"Don't bother," she said.

They slept late into Sunday morning, and when he drew the curtain a few inches to check the weather, he saw the terra-cotta oven on its side, the lid in two pieces.

"Bloody foxes," he said quietly, not sure if Martha was awake or not. "Or bloody cats. Or bloody squirrels. Bloody nature anyway." He stood at the window, uncertain whether to get back into bed, or go downstairs and slowly start another day.

# At Phil & Joanna's 3:
# Look, No Hands

FOR ONCE, it was warm enough to eat outside, around a table whose slatted top was beginning to buckle. Candles in tin lanterns had been lit from the start, and were now becoming useful. We had talked about Obama's first hundred days and more, his abandonment of torture as an instrument of state, British complicity in extraterritorial rendition, bankers' bonuses, and how long it would be to the next general election. We had tried comparing the threatened swine-flu outbreak to the avian flu that never arrived, but lacked anyone approaching an epidemiologist. Now, a silence fell.

"I was thinking . . . last time we all foregathered—"

"Before this groaning board—"

"Set before us by—quick, give me some clichés . . ."

"Mine host."

"A veritable Trimalchio."

"Mistress Quickly."

"No good. So—Phil and Joanna, let's call them that, the epitomes of hostliness."

"That tongue, by the way . . ."

"Was it *tongue*? You said it was beef."

"Well, it was. Tongue *is* beef. Ox tongue, calves' tongue."

"But . . . but I don't *like* tongue. It's been in a dead cow's mouth."

"And last time you were here, you were telling us about sending valentines, you two . . . married turtledoves. And about the friend of yours who was going to have her stomach stapled for when her husband came home."

"It was liposuction, actually."

"And someone asked, was that love or vanity?"

"Female insecurity, I think was the alternative."

"Point of information. Was this before her bloke had his radical testoctomy or whatever it's called?"

"Oh, ages before. And anyway, she didn't have it done."

"Didn't she?"

"I thought I told you that."

"But we talked about—what was that phrase of Dick's?—posterior intromission."

"Well, she didn't have it done. I'm sure I said."

"And—to return to my point—someone asked if any of us felt up to making love after getting home from here."

"A question which went very largely unanswered."

"Is that where you're taking us, David, with this Socratic preface?"

"No. Maybe yes. No, not exactly."

"Lead on, Macduff."

"This feels to me like when you have a collection of blokes round a table and someone mentions how the size of your tackle is directly related . . . Dick, why are you putting your hands out of sight?"

"Because I know the end of the sentence. And because, frankly, I don't want to embarrass anyone by obliging them to deduce the magnificence of my, as you put it, tackle."

"Sue, a question. The class has in its last lesson been taught the difference between a simile and a metaphor. Now, which grammatical term would you say best described the comparison between the size of a man's hands and the size of his tackle?"

"Is there a grammatical term called boasting?"

"There's that term for comparing the smaller to the greater. The part to the whole. Litotes? Hendiadys? Anacoluthon?"

"They all sound like Greek holiday resorts to me."

"As I was trying to say, we don't talk about love."

". . ."

". . ."

". . ."

". . ."

". . ."

". . ."

"So that's my point."

"A friend of mine once said he didn't think it was possible to be happy for longer than two weeks at any one stretch."

"Who was this miserable bastard?"

"A friend of mine."

"Very suspicious."

"Why?"

"Well, *a friend of mine*—anyone remember Matthew? Yes, no? He was a great *coureur de femmes*."

"Translation, please."

"Oh, he fucked for England. Amazing energy. And constant . . . interest. Anyway, there was a time when—how shall I put this—well, when women started using their hands, their fingers, on themselves while they were having sex."

"When exactly would you date this to?"

"Between the end of the Chatterley ban and the Beatles' first LP?"

"No, since you ask. Later. Seventies, more like . . ."

"And Matthew noticed this . . . sociodigital change sooner than most, being more diligent in the fieldwork, and he decided to raise it with a woman he knew—not a girlfriend or an ex, but someone he could always talk to. A confidante. And so, over a drink, he said to her casually, 'A friend of mine told me the other day that he'd noticed women using their hands more when having sex.' And this woman replied, 'Well, your friend must have a really small dick. Or not be much good at using it.'"

"Collapse of stout party, eh?"

"He died. Youngish. Brain tumour."

"A friend of mine—"

"Is that 'a friend of mine' or '*a friend of mine*'?"

"Will. Remember him? He got cancer. He was a great drinker, a great smoker and a great womaniser. And I remember where the cancer had reached by the time they discovered it: liver, lungs, urethra."

"The grammatical term for that is: poetic justice."

"But it was weird, wasn't it?"

"Are you saying Matthew died of a brain tumour because he fucked a lot? How does that work?"

"Maybe he had sex on the brain."

"The worst place to have it, as one sage remarked."

"Love."

"Bless you. *Gesundheit.*"

"I read somewhere that in France, when a chap's flies were undone, another chap's polite way of drawing attention to it was to say, '*Vive l'Empereur.*' Not that I've ever heard anyone say it. Or really understood it."

"Maybe the end of your knob is meant to look like the top of Napoleon's head."

"Speak for yourself."

"Or that hat he always wears in cartoons."

"I hate that word 'knob.' I hate it even more as a verb than a noun. 'He knobbed her.' Eurch."

"Love."

"  . . .  "

"  . . .  "

"  . . .  "

"Good. I'm glad I've got your attention. It's what we don't talk about. Love."

"Whoa. Steady on, old chap. Mustn't frighten the horses and all that."

"Larry will bear me out. As our resident alien."

"You know, when I first came over here, the things I noticed most were how you were always making jokes, and how often you use the C-word."

"Don't you use the C-word in America?"

"I guess we certainly avoid it in the presence of women."

"How very peculiar. And richly ironic, if you don't mind my saying."

"But, Larry, you prove my point. We make jokes instead of being serious, and we talk about sex instead of talking about love."

"I think jokes are a good way of being serious. Often the best way."

"Only an Englishman would think that, or say that."

"Are you wanting me to apologise for being English, or something?"

"Don't get so defensive."

"Are you calling me a cunt, by any chance?"

"Men talk about sex, women talk about love."

"Bollocks."

"Well, why hasn't a woman spoken in the last however many minutes?"

"I was wondering if the size of a woman's hands was related to the amount she has to use them in bed with her husband."

"Dick, shut the fuck up."

"Boys. Shh. Neighbours. Voices carry much more at this time of night."

"Joanna, tell us what you think."

"Why me?"

"Because I asked."

"Very well. I don't think there was a time—not in my life, anyway—when men and women sat around in a group talking about love. It's true we talk about sex a lot more—or rather, we listen to you talk about sex a lot more. I also think—well, it's practically a cliché now—that if women knew how men talked about them behind their backs they wouldn't find it very elevating. And if men knew how women talked about them behind their backs—"

"It'd be dick-shrivelling."

"Women can fake it, men can't. It's the law of the jungle."

"The law of the jungle is rape, not faked orgasm."

"A human being is the only creature which can reflect upon its own existence, conceive of its own death, and fake orgasm. We're not God's special ones for nothing."

"A man can fake orgasm."

"Really? Willing to share the secret?"

"A woman doesn't always know if a man has come. From internal feeling, I mean."

"That's another hands-under-the-table moment."

"Well, a man can't fake *erection*, anyway."

"The cock never lies."

"The sun also rises."

"What's the connection?"

"Oh, both sound like book titles. Only one is."

"Actually, the cock does lie."

"Are we sure we want to go there?"

"First-night nerves. It's not that you don't want to, it's just that your cock lets you down. It lies."

"Love."

"An old friend of ours—she's a New Yorker—worked as a lawyer for years and years—decided to retrain by going to film school. She was in her fifties already. And she found herself surrounded by kids thirty years younger than her. And she used to listen to them, and sometimes they confided in her about their lives, and you know what she concluded? That they didn't think twice about going to bed with someone, but they were really, really scared of getting close, or of anyone getting close to them."

"The point being?"

"They were afraid of love. Afraid of . . . dependency. Or having someone dependent on them. Or both."

"Afraid of pain."

"Afraid of anything that would interfere with their careers, more like. You know, New York . . ."

"Maybe. But I think Sue's right. Afraid of pain."

"Last time—or the time before—someone was asking if there was cancer of the heart. Of course there is. And it's called love."

"Do I hear distant drums and ape calls?"

"My condolences to your spouse."

"Come on. Stop being facetious. Stop thinking about who you're married to or who you're sitting next to. Think about what love's been like in your life, and think about it in other people's lives."

"And?"

"Pain."

"No gain without pain, as they say."

"I've known pain where there's no gain. In most cases, actually. 'Suffering ennobles'—I've always known that was a moralistic lie. Suffering diminishes the individual. Pain degrades."

"Well, I've been hurt—I am in pain—because last time we were here I was telling you in a very discreet way about my home bum-cancer screening . . ."

"Which you said you did on St. Valentine's Day."

"And no bugger or C-word here has actually had the courtesy to enquire if I got the result."

"Dick, did you get the result?"

"Yes, a letter from someone whose job title beneath the illegible signature was, if you can credit it, hub director."

"We won't go there."

"And he was writing to say that my result was normal."

"A-*ha*."

"That's great, Dick."

"And then—new paragraph—the letter went on to say, and I quote from memory—though, what else might one quote from?—that, *quote*, no screening test is one hundred percent accurate, so a normal result does not guarantee that you do not have, or will never develop, bowel cancer."

"Well, they couldn't *guarantee*, could they?"

"It's all about getting sued."

"Everything's about getting sued nowadays."

"Hence, for example, the prenup—to get us back on track a bit. Larry, would you say the prenup is a proof of love or of insecurity?"

"I don't know, I've never signed one. I guess it's usually lawyers protecting family money. Maybe it doesn't have anything to do with how you feel, it's just social protocol. Like pretending you believe all the words of the marriage service."

"I did. Every single one."

"'With my body I thee roger'—ah, now *that* takes me back. Oh dear, Joanna's looking a little balefully at me again."

"Cancer of the heart, not the bum, is the topic."

"You're maintaining Love Is Pain, are you, Joanna?"

"No. I'm just thinking of a few people—men, yes, they are all men, actually—who've never been hurt by love. Who are, in fact, incapable of being hurt by love. Who set up a system of evasion and control that guarantees they'll never get hurt."

"Is that so unreasonable? It sounds like the emotional equivalent of a prenup."

"It may be *reasonable*, but that confirms my point. Some men can do the whole thing—sex, marriage, fatherhood, companionship—and not feel any real pain. Frustration, embarrassment, boredom, anger . . . and that's it. Their idea of pain is when a woman doesn't repay dinner with sex."

"Who said men were more cynical than women?"

"I'm not being cynical. We can all name a couple of people like that."

"You mean you're not in love unless you're in pain?"

"Of course I don't mean that. I just mean that, well, it's like jealousy. Love can't exist without the possibility of jealousy. If you're lucky, you may never feel it, but if the possibility, the capacity to feel it, isn't there, then you aren't in love. And it's the same with pain."

"So Dick wasn't off the point after all?"

". . . ?"

"Well, he doesn't have bum cancer, except there's a possibility he might, either now or in the future."

"Thank you. Vindicated. I knew I knew what I was really talking about."

"You and the hub director."

"You're talking about Pete, aren't you?"

"Who's Pete? The hub director?"

"No, Pete's the no-pain guy."

"Pete's one of those counters. You know, how many women. He could name the day he hit double figures, name the day it was fifty."

"Well, we're all counters."

"Are we?"

"Yes, I remember very well getting to two."

"There were quite a lot of halves with me, if you know what I mean."

"All too well. Now there's pain for you."

"No, that's what Pete would call pain. It's just hurt pride. He does hurt pride and high anxiety. That's as close as he gets to pain."

"Sensible guy. What's not to like? Did he ever marry?"

"Twice. Out of both of them now."

"And?"

"Embarrassment, a certain self-pity, weariness. But nothing stronger."

"So according to you he's never loved?"

"Indeed."

"But he wouldn't say that. He'd say he'd been in love. More than once."

"Yes, he'd probably say dozens of times."

"'It's the hypocrisy I can't stand.'"

"I'll never live down saying that, will I?"

"Well, maybe it's good enough."

"What is?"

"To believe you've been in love, or are in love. Isn't that just as good?"

"Not if it isn't true."

"Hang on. Isn't there a bit of rank-pulling going on here? 'Only we've been in love because only we've suffered.'"

"I wasn't saying that."

"Weren't you?"

"Do you think women love more than men?"

"More—in the sense of more often or more intensely?"

"Only a man could ask that question."

"Well, that's what I am—a poor fucking man."

"Not after dinner at Phil and Joanna's, you aren't. As we noted."

"Did we?"

"Oh God, I hope you're not going to make us all go home and try to get it on to prove—"

"I hate 'get it on' as well."

"I remember one of those American TV shows—you know, we solve your emotional and sexual problems by putting you in front of a studio audience and making a spectacle out of you, and sending the audience home feeling very glad they aren't you."

"That's an extremely British denunciation."

"Well, I remain British. Anyway, there was this woman, talking about how her marriage or relationship wasn't working, and of course they got onto sex right away, and one of the so-called experts, some glib TV counsellor, actually asked her, 'Do you have big orgasms?'"

"Ker-pow. Straight for the G-spot."

"And she looked at this therapist, and said, with actually rather a fetching modesty, 'Well, they seem big to me.'"

"Bravo. And so say all of us."

"So what are you saying?"

"I'm saying we shouldn't necessarily feel superior to Pete."

"Do we? I don't. And if he's passed the fifty mark, I doff my cap."

"Do you think Pete gets off with women because he can't get on with them?"

"No, I just think he has a low boredom threshold."

"If you're in love, you don't have a boredom threshold."

"I think you can be in love and bored."

"Do I fear another hands-under-the-table moment?"

"Don't be so defensive."

"Well, I am. I come here to gorge myself on your delicious food and wine, not to be water-boarded like this."

"Sing for your supper."

"'And you'll get breakfast . . .'"

"What I'm saying, in defence of this Pete whom I've never met, is merely, perhaps he's loved, or been in love, as much as his constitution allows, and why feel superior to him just because of that?"

"There are some people who wouldn't fall in love if they hadn't read about it first."

"Spare us your Froggy wisdom for one night."

"Is it safe to take our hands out from under the table now?"

"It's never safe. That's the whole point."

"What *is* the point, by the way?"

"Let me summarise. For those unable to keep up. This house is agreed that the British use the C-word far too liberally, that men talk about sex because they can't talk about love, that women and the Frogs understand love better than Englishmen, that love is pain, and that any man who's had more women than me, apart from being a lucky cunt, doesn't really understand women."

"Brilliant, Dick. I second the motion."

"You second Dick's motion? You must be the hub director."

"Oh, shut up, boys. I thought that was a very male summary."

"Would you like to give us a female summary?"

"Probably not."

"Are you implying that summarising is a contemptible male trait?"

"Not especially. Though my summary might mention how passive-aggressive men get when talking about subjects which make them feel unsure of themselves."

"'Passive-aggressive.' I hate that word, or phrase, or whatever it is. I would guess it has a ninety to ninety-five percent female use. I don't even know what it means. Or rather, what it's meant to mean."

"What did we say before we said 'passive-aggressive'?"

"How about 'well mannered'?"

"'Passive-aggressive' indicates a psychological condition."

"So does 'well mannered.' And a very healthy one too."

"Does anyone seriously think—if we were to pass the met-aphorical port at this stage and the ladies were to retire—that they'd sit around talking about love and we'd sit around talking about sex?"

"When I was a boy, before I knew anything about girls, I used to look forward to them equally."

"You mean, boys *and* girls?"

"Cunt. No, love and sex."

"*Voices*. Keep them down."

"Is there anything to match that, do you think, in the field of human emotional endeavour? The force of longing for sex and love when you haven't had either?"

"I remember it all too well. Life just seemed . . . impossible. Now *that* was pain."

"And yet it didn't turn out so badly. We've all had love and sex, sometimes even at the same time."

"And now we're going to put on our coats and go home and have one or the other and next time there will be a show of hands."

"Or a hiding of hands."

"Boys never stop being boys, do they?"

"Does that qualify as passive-aggressive?"

"I can do active-aggressive if you'd prefer."

"Leave it, sweetie."

"You know, this is one evening when I don't want to be the first to go."

"Let's all go together, then Phil and Joanna can discuss us while they clear up."

"Actually, we don't do that."

"You don't?"

"No, we have a ritual. Phil clears, I stack the dishwasher. We put on some music. I wash up the stuff that won't go in the dishwasher, Phil dries. We don't discuss you."

"What charming hosts. A veritable Trimalchio and Mistress Quickly."

"What Jo means is, we're all talked out. We discuss you tomorrow, over breakfast. And lunch. And, in this instance, probably dinner as well."

"Phil, you old bastard."

"I trust no one's driving."

"I don't trust anyone's driving either. Only my own."

"You're not really?"

"I'm not a complete idiot. We're all walking or cabbing it."

"Actually, we're going to stand on the pavement discussing you two for a while."

"Was that really tongue, by the way?"

"Sure."

"But I don't like tongue."

After he had closed the front door, Phil put on some Madeleine Peyroux, kissed his wife on the apron string round the back of her neck, went upstairs to a darkened bedroom, cautiously approached the window, saw the others standing on the pavement, and watched them until they dispersed.

# Trespass

WHEN HE and Cath broke up, he thought about joining the Ramblers, but it seemed too obviously sad a thing to do. He imagined the conversation:

"Hi, Geoff. Sorry to hear about you and Cath. How're you doing?"

"Oh, fine, thanks. I've joined the Ramblers."

"Good move."

He could see the rest of it too: getting the magazine, studying the open-to-all invitation—meet 10:30, Saturday 12th, in car park immed. SE of Methodist Chapel—cleaning his boots the night before, cutting an extra sandwich just in case, maybe taking an extra tangerine as well, and turning up at the car park with (despite all his warnings to himself) a hopeful heart. A hopeful heart waiting to be bruised. And then it would be a case of getting through the walk, saying cheery farewells, and going home to eat the leftover sandwich and tangerine for his supper. Now that would be sad.

Of course, he carried on walking. Most weekends, in most weathers, he'd be out with his boots and pack, his water bottle and his map. Nor was he going to keep away from all the walks he'd done with Cath. They weren't "their" walks, after all; and if they were, he'd be reclaiming them by doing them by himself. She didn't own the circuit from Calver: along the Derwent, through Froggatt Woods to Grindleford, perhaps a diversion to the Grouse Inn for lunch, then along past the Bronze Age stone circle, lost in summer months amid the bracken, all leading to the grand surprise of Curbar Edge. She didn't own that, nobody did.

Afterwards, he made a note in his walking log: 2 hrs 45 mns. With Cath it used to take 3 hrs 30 mns, and an extra 30 mns if they went to the Grouse for a sandwich. That was one of the things about being single again: you saved time. You walked quicker, you got home and drank a beer quicker, you ate your supper quicker. And then the sex you had with yourself, that was quicker too. You gained all this extra time, Geoff thought—extra time in which to be lonely. Stop that, he said to himself. You aren't allowed to be a sad person; you're only allowed to be sad.

"I thought we were going to get married."

"That's why we aren't," Cath had replied.

"I don't understand."

"No, you don't."

"Will you please explain?"

"No."

"Why not?"

"Because that's the whole point. If you can't see, if I have to explain—that's why we're not getting married."

"You're not being logical."

"I'm also not getting married."

Forget it, forget it, it's gone. On the one hand, she liked you making the decisions; on the other hand, she found you controlling. On the one hand, she liked living with you; on the other, she didn't want to go on living with you. On the one hand, she knew you'd be a good father; on the other, she didn't want to have your children. Logic, right? Forget it.

"Hello." He surprised himself. He didn't say hello to women he didn't know in the lunch queue. He only said hello to women he didn't know on walking paths, when you got a nod or a smile or a lifted trekking pole in reply. But—actually, he did know her.

"You're from the bank."

"Right."

"Lynn."

"Very good."

A small moment of genius, remembering her plastic name tag through the bulletproof glass. And she was having the vegetarian lasagne as well. Did she mind . . . ? No, fine. There was only one free table. And it was just sort of easy. He knew she worked in the bank, she knew he taught at the school. She'd moved to the town a couple of months previously, and no, she hadn't been up to the Tor yet. Would she be OK in trainers?

The next Saturday she wore jeans and a sweater; she seemed half-amused, half-alarmed as he got his boots and pack out of the car and pulled on his scarlet mesh-lined Gore-tex jacket.

"You'll need water."

"Will I?"

"Unless you don't mind sharing."

She nodded; they set off. As they climbed out of the town, the view broadened to include both her bank and his school. He let her set the pace. She walked easily. He wanted to ask how old she was, whether she went to the gym, and say how she looked taller than when sitting down behind the glass. Instead, he pointed out the ruins of an old slate-works and the rare breed of sheep—Jacobs, were they?—that Jim Henderson had been farming since people down south started wanting lamb that didn't taste like lamb, and were happy to pay for it.

Halfway up it began to drizzle, and he grew anxious about her trainers on the wet shale near the top. He stopped, unzipped his pack, and gave her a spare waterproof. She took it as if it was quite normal that he'd brought it. He liked that. She also didn't ask whose it was, who'd left it behind.

He passed her the water bottle; she drank and wiped the rim.

"What else have you got in there?"

"Sandwiches, tangerines. Unless you want to turn back."

"As long as you haven't got a pair of those awful plastic trousers."

"No."

He did, of course. And not just his own, but a pair of Cath's he'd brought for her. Something in him, something bold and timid at the same time, wanted to say, "Actually, I'm wearing North Cape Coolmax boxers with the single-button fly."

After they started sleeping together, he took her to the Great Outdoors. They got her boots—a pair of Brasher Supalites—and, as she stood up in them, walked tentatively to a mirror and back, then did a little tap dance, he thought how incredibly sexy small female feet could look in walking boots. They got her three pairs of ergonomic trekking socks designed to absorb pressure peaks, and she widened her eyes at the idea of socks having a left and a right like shoes. Three pairs of inner socks too. They got her a day pack, or a day sack, as the hunky assistant preferred to call it, by which point Geoff felt the fellow beginning to get out of line. He'd shown Lynn how to position the hip belt, tighten the shoulder straps and adjust the top tensioners; now he was patting the pack and juggling it up and down in far too intimate a way.

"And a water bottle," Geoff said firmly, to cut all that off.

They got her a waterproof jacket in a dark green that set off the flame of her hair; then he waited and let Hunk suggest water-proof trousers and get laughed at in reply. At the cash desk he handed over his credit card.

"No, you can't."

"I'd like to. I'd really like to."

"But why?"

"I'd like to. Must be your birthday soon. Well, sometime in the next twelve months. Got to be."

"Thank you," Lynn said, but he could tell she was a bit edgy about it. "Will you wrap them up again for my birthday?"

"I'll do more than that. I'll clean your Brashers specially. Oh yes," he said to the cashier, "and we'd better have some polish. Classic Brown, please."

Before they went walking next, he dubbined her boots to make the leather supple and strengthen the waterproofing. As he slipped his hand inside the fresh-smelling Brashers, he noted again, as he had in the shop, that she took half a size smaller than Cath. Half a size? It felt like a full size to him.

They did Hathersage and Padley Chapel; Calke Abbey and Staunton Harold; Dove Dale as it narrows and deepens to Milldale; Lathkill Dale from Alport to Ricklow Quarry; Cromford Canal and the High Peak Trail. They climbed out of Hope to Lose Hill, then along what he promised her was the most scenic ridge walk in the entire Peak District, until they came to Mam Tor, where the paragliders gathered: huge men who sweated up the hill with vast packs on their backs, then spread out their canopies like laundry on the grassy slope and waited for the upcurrent to lift them off their feet and into the sky.

"Isn't that thrilling," she said. "Wouldn't you like to do that?"

Geoff thought of men in hospital wards with broken backs, of paraplegics and quadriplegics. He thought of midair collisions with light aircraft. He thought of not being able to control the wind and getting carried higher and higher into the cloud, of coming down in unknown landscape, of getting lost and scared and peeing yourself. Of not having your boots on a path and a map in your hand.

"Sort of," he replied.

For him, freedom lay on the ground. He told her about the trespass on Kinder Scout in the 1930s: how walkers and hikers had come out from Manchester in their hundreds to the Duke of Devonshire's grouse moors to protest against lack of access to the countryside; how it had been a peaceful day except when a drunken gamekeeper shot himself with his own gun; how the trespass had led to the creation of national parks and registered rights of way; and how the man who'd led it had died recently, but there was still one survivor, now 103, living in a Methodist old people's home not far away. Geoff thought his story soared better than any bloody paraglider.

"They just went trampling across his land like that?"

"Not trampling. Tramping, perhaps." Geoff was pleased with this emendation.

"But it *was* his land?"

"Technically, yes. Historically, perhaps not."

"Are you a socialist?"

"I'm in favour of the right to roam," he said cautiously. He didn't want to put a foot wrong now.

"It's all right. I wouldn't mind. Either way."

"What are you?"

"I don't vote."

Emboldened, he said, "I'm Labour."

"I thought you would be."

In his walking log, he noted the routes they took, the date, the weather, the duration, ending with an L in red for Lynn. As opposed to a blue C for Cath. Times were about the same, regardless of the initial.

Should he get her a trekking pole? He didn't want to push it—she'd refused all offers of a walking hat, despite having the pros and cons explained to her. Not that there were any cons. Still, better a bare head than a baseball cap. He really couldn't take a walker in a baseball cap seriously, male or female.

He could get her a compass. Except he already had one himself, and rarely consulted it. If ever he broke his ankle, and had to tell her through the pain to set off across the moor using that tumbledown sheepfold as a reference point and keep heading NNE—showing her how to turn the instrument and set a course—then she could have his for the purpose. No, one compass between two, that was right, somehow. Symbolic, you could say.

They did the Kinder Downfall circuit: Bowden Bridge car park, the reservoir, pick up the Pennine Way to the Downfall, fork right at Red Brook and down past Tunstead House and the Kinderstones. He told her about the average rainfall, and how when it froze the Downfall turned into a cascade of icicles. One of the sights for the winter walker.

She didn't answer. Well, anyway, they'd have to get her a fleece if they were going up two thousand feet in winter. He still had the issue of *Country Walking* with the fleece test in it.

In the car park he looked at his watch.

"Are we late for something?"

"No, just checking. Four and a quarter."

"Is that good or bad?"

"It's good because I'm with you."

It was also good because four and a quarter is what it used to take him and Cath, and say what you will, Cath was one pretty fit walker.

Lynn lit a Silk Cut, as she did at the end of every walk. She didn't smoke much, and he didn't really mind, even if he thought it was a pretty stupid habit. Just when she'd done her cardio-vascular system a power of good . . . Still, he knew from being a teacher that there were times when you had to confront, and times when you took a less direct route.

"We could go up again after Christmas. In the New Year." Yes, he could get her the fleece as her present.

She looked at him, and took a deep puff on her cigarette.

"If the weather got cold enough, that is. For the icicles."

"Geoff," she said. "You're on my space."

"I just—"

"You're on my space."

"Yes, Miss Duke of Devonshire."

But she didn't think that was funny, and they drove home mainly in silence. Perhaps he'd walked her too hard. It was a bit of a stiff pull, a thousand feet or more.

He'd put the pizzas in the oven, laid the table, and was just pulling the tab on his first beer when she said,

"Look, it's June. We met in—February?"

"Jan. twenty-ninth," he replied, automatically, as he did when a pupil mistakenly guessed 1079 for the Battle of Hastings.

"January the twenty-ninth," she repeated. "Look, I don't think I can do Christmas."

"Of course. You've got family."

"No, I don't mean I've got family. Of course I've got family. I mean, I can't do Christmas."

When Geoff was faced with what, despite principled beliefs to the contrary, he nonetheless could only regard as gross female illogicality, he tended to go silent. One minute you were steaming along a track, the weight on your shoulders barely noticeable, and then suddenly you were in a pathless scrubland with no waymarks, the mist descending and the ground boggy beneath your feet.

But she didn't go on, so he tried helping her. "Don't much like Christmas myself. All that eating and drinking. Still—"

"Who knows where I'll be at Christmas."

"You mean, the bank might transfer you?" He hadn't thought of that.

"Geoff, listen. We met in January, as you pointed out. Things are . . . fine. I'm having a nice time, a nice enough time . . ."

"Gotcha. Right." It was that stuff again, that stuff he didn't seem to be getting any better at. "No, course not. Didn't mean. Anyway, I'll turn the oven up. Crispy base." He took a swig of his beer.

"It's just—"

"Don't say it. I know. I get you." He was going to add "Miss Duke of Devonshire" again, but he didn't, and later, thinking it over, he guessed it wouldn't have helped.

In September, he persuaded her to take a day's leave so they could do the circuit from Calver. It was best to avoid the week-end, when every hiker and rock climber would be crawling over Curbar Edge.

They parked in the cul-de-sac next to the Bridge Inn and set off, passing Calver Mill on the other side of the Derwent.

"Richard Arkwright is supposed to have built that," he said. "Seventeen eighty-five, I think."

"It's not a mill anymore."

"No, well, as you see. Offices. Maybe residential. Or a bit of both."

They followed the river, past the thrashing weir, through Froggatt and then Froggatt Woods to Grindleford. As they came out of the woods, the autumn sun, though weak, made him glad of his hat. Lynn still refused to buy one, and he supposed he wouldn't mention it again until the spring. She'd taken a tan these summer months, and her freckles showed more than when he'd first met her.

There was a sharp climb out of Grindleford, which she took without a murmur; then he led the way across a field to the Grouse Inn. They sat up at the bar for a sandwich. Afterwards, the barman muttered, "Coffee?" She said "Yes" and he said "No." He didn't believe in coffee on a walk. You just needed water against dehydration. Coffee was a stimulant and the whole . . . theory was that the walk should be stimulating enough with-out any assistance. Alcohol: stupid. He'd even come across hikers smoking joints.

He told her some of this, which may have been a mistake, because she said, "I'm only having a coffee, right?"—and then lit up a Silk Cut. Not waiting till the end of the walk. She looked at him.

"Yes?"

"I didn't say anything."

"You don't need to."

Geoff sighed. "I forgot to point out the signpost as we got to Grindleford. It's antique. Nearly a hundred years old. Not many left in the Peak District."

She blew smoke at him, rather deliberately, it seemed.

"And, all right, I also read somewhere that low-tar cigarettes are in fact just as bad for you because they make you inhale more deeply to get the nicotine, so actually you're taking more of the toxins into your lungs."

"Then I may as well switch back to Marlboro Lights."

They retraced their steps, picked up the path again, crossed a road and took a left by the sign for the Eastern Moors Estate.

"Is this where the Bronze Age circle is?"

"I think so."

"What does that mean?"

Fair enough. But also, there's no point in not being yourself, is there? He was thirty-one, he had his opinions, he knew stuff.

"The circle is coming up on the left-hand side. But I don't think we should look at it this time."

"This time?"

"It's in the bracken."

"You mean you can't see it properly."

"No, I don't mean that. Well, yes, you do see it better at other times of the year. What I mean is that between August and October it's inadvisable to walk in bracken. Or downwind of it, for that matter."

"You're going to tell me why, aren't you?"

"Since you ask. If you walk in bracken for ten minutes, you're liable to ingest anything up to fifty thousand spores. They're too large to go into your lungs, so they go into your stomach. Tests have found them to be carcinogenic to animals."

"Lucky cows don't smoke as well."

"There are also ticks that transmit Lyme disease, which . . ."

"So?"

"So if you have to walk in bracken, you tuck your trousers into your socks, roll your sleeves down, and wear a face mask."

"A face mask?"

"Respro makes one." Well, she'd asked, and she was getting the bloody answer. "It's called the Respro Bandit face scarf."

When she was sure he'd finished, she said, "Thank you. Now lend me your handkerchief."

She tucked her trousers in, rolled her sleeves down, tied his hankie bandit-style around her face, and tramped off into the bracken. He waited upwind. Another thing you could do was get some Bug Proof, and put it on your trousers and socks. It killed the ticks on contact. Not that he'd tried it. Yet.

When she returned they set off in silence along the gritstone edge which was either called Froggatt Edge or Curbar Edge, or both, he didn't care either way for the moment. The turf was springy up here, and reached right to the point where the ground dropped away sheer for what looked like several hundred feet. It was always a surprise: without any sense of having climbed much, you found yourself startlingly high, miles above the sunlit valley with its tiny villages. You didn't need to be a bloody paraglider to get a view like this. There had been quarries around here, from which many of the country's millstones came. But he didn't tell her that.

He loved this spot. The first time he came here, he was looking down at the valley, no one visible for miles, and all of a sudden a helmeted face popped up at his feet, and a bearded climber was hauling himself from nowhere up onto the turf. Life was full of surprises, wasn't it? Edge climbers, potholers, paragliders. People thought that if you were up in the air, you were as free as a bloody bird. Well, you weren't. There were rules there too, like everywhere. Lynn, in his opinion, was standing too close to the edge.

Geoff didn't say anything. He didn't, for that matter, feel anything. Puzzled, of course, but that would pass. He set off again, unconcerned whether she was following or not. Another half mile of this high upland, then a sharpish descent back to Calver. He had begun thinking about next week's work when he heard her scream.

He ran back, his pack thumping, the water in his bottle audibly sloshing.

"Christ, are you OK? Is it your foot? I should have told you about the rabbit holes."

But she just looked at him, expressionlessly. In shock, probably.

"Are you hurt?"

"No."

"Did you twist your ankle?"

"No."

He looked down at her Brasher Supalites: bracken caught in the eyelets, and the morning's shine gone from them. "Sorry—don't understand."

"What?"

"Why you screamed."

"Because I felt like it."

Ah, missing waymarks again. "And . . . why did you feel like it?"

"Because I did."

No, he must have misheard, or misunderstood, or something. "Look, sorry, maybe I walked you too hard—"

"I'm fine, I said."

"Was it because—"

"I told you, I felt like it."

They walked away from the gritstone edge and then down, in silence, to where they'd left the car. As he began unlacing his boots, she lit a cigarette. Well, he was sorry, but he was going to get to the bottom of it.

"Was it something to do with me?"

"No, it was something to do with me. I'm the one who screamed."

"Do you feel like doing it again? Now?"

"What do you mean?"

"I mean, if you felt like screaming again, now, what would it feel like?"

"Geoff, it would feel like wanting to scream again, now."

"And when do you think you'll do it again?"

She didn't answer that, and neither of them was surprised. She stamped out her Silk Cut beneath a Supalite, and began to undo the laces, flicking bits of bracken onto the tarmac.

"4 hrs inc lunch Grouse," he wrote in his walking log. "Weather fine." He added a red L in the final column, beneath a constant vertical of red Ls. In bed, that night, he slept diagonally, and jolly good luck to him, he thought. The next morning, over breakfast, he leafed through a copy of Country Walking and filled out the application form to join the Ramblers. It said he could pay either by cheque or direct debit. He thought about this for a while, and chose direct debit.

# At Phil & Joanna's 4:
# One in Five

IT WAS LATE October, but Phil was determined to light a fire with some apple logs they'd brought back from the country. The chimney, rarely used, didn't draw fully, and from time to time aromatic smoke drifted back into the room. We had talked yet again about bankers' bonuses and Obama's continuing troubles, and the fact that the mayor of London didn't seem to have decommissioned any bendy buses, so were almost relieved to get onto the subject of Joanna's new maplewood work surface.

"No, it's good-looking and really hard-wearing."

"Like the rest of us."

"Do you have to oil it a lot?"

"There's a formula: once a day for a week, once a week for a month, once a month for a year, and thereafter whenever you feel like it."

"Sounds like the formula for married sex."

"Dick, you beast."

"No wonder you got married so often, my friend."

"Which reminds me—"

"Don't you think those are the three most sinister words in the English language—'Which reminds me'?"

". . . are we going to report on the homework we were set last time?"

"Homework?"

"Whether you made the beast with two backs when you got home."

"Were we meant to? I don't remember."

"Oh, let's skip this."

"Yes, do you mind if we have a moratorium on sex talk just for one evening?"

"Only if you first answer the following question. Do you think—present company excepted—that people lie more about sex than about anything else?"

"Is that supposed to be the case?"

"There's good anecdotal evidence, I'd say."

"And, I think, scientific evidence."

"You mean, people admitting to social surveys that they'd lied about sex in previous surveys?"

"There's no one else present, after all."

"Not unless you go dogging."

"Dogging?"

"Don't you have that in the States, Larry? A couple doing it in the car in a lay-by or somewhere public, so that other people can creep up and watch. It's an old English custom, like morris dancing."

"Well, maybe in West Virginia . . ."

"OK, that's enough, boys."

"The wider point is, how would we know if they were telling the truth?"

"How do we know anything's true?"

"Is that a high-philosophical question?"

"More a low-practical one. In general. How do we know exactly? I remember some intellectual on the radio discussing the start of the Second World War, and coming to the conclusion that all you could say for certain was, 'Something happened.' I was very struck by that."

"Oh, come on. We'll be in Did Six Million Die? territory at

this rate. Or, the moon-landing shots were faked because of that supposedly impossible shadow. Or, 9/11 was planned by the Bush administration."

"Well, only fascists question the first and only nutters believe the second."

"And the 9/11 attacks couldn't have been planned by the Bush administration because they didn't go wrong."

"Larry goes native—a joke, and a cynical one at that. Congratulations."

"When in Rome . . ."

"No, what I'm talking about is why we, as nonfascist non-nutters, believe what we believe."

"Believe what?"

"Anything from two plus two equals four to God's in his heaven and all's right with the world."

"But we don't believe all's right with the world or that God's in his heaven. On the contrary."

"Then why do we believe the contrary?"

"Either because we've worked it out for ourselves or because experts tell us it's the case."

"But why do we believe the experts we believe?"

"Because we trust them."

"Why do we trust them?"

"Well, I trust Galileo more than the pope, so I believe the earth goes round the sun."

"But we don't trust Galileo himself, for the simple reason that we've none of us read his proof. I'm assuming that's the case. So who or what we're trusting is a second level of experts."

"Who probably know even more than Galileo."

"Here's a paradox. We all of us read a newspaper, and most of us believe most of what our newspaper tells us. But at the same time every survey says that journalists are generally regarded as untrustworthy. Down there at the bottom with estate agents."

"It's other people's newspapers that are untrustworthy. Ours are reliable."

"Some genius once wrote that any sentence beginning 'One in five of us believes or thinks such-and-such' is automatically suspect. And the sentence that is least likely to be true is one beginning 'Perhaps as many as one in five . . .'"

"Who was this genius?"

"A journalist."

"You know that thing about surveillance cameras? How Britain's supposed to have more of them per head of population than anywhere else in the world? We all know that, don't we? So, there was a rebuttal in the paper by a journalist who said it was all hooey and paranoia, and went on to prove it, or try to. But he didn't prove it to me because he's one of those journalists I always disagree with anyway. So I refused to believe he could be right about this. And then I wondered if I didn't believe him because I *want* to live in a country with the largest amount of surveillance cameras. And then I couldn't work out whether that was because it made me feel safer, or because I somehow rather enjoyed feeling paranoid."

"So where is the point or the line at which reasonable people stop assuming truth and start doubting it?"

"Isn't there usually an accumulation of evidence leading to doubt?"

"Like, the husband is always the first to suspect and the last to know."

"Or the wife."

"*Mutatis mutandis.*"

"*In propria persona.*"

"That's another thing about the British. Well, your kind of British. The Latin you speak."

"Do we?"

"I guess we do. *Homo homini lupus.*"

"Et tu, Brute."

"And in case you think we're showing off our education, we aren't. It's more despair. We're probably the last generation to have these phrases at our disposal. They don't have classical references in the Times crossword anymore. Or Shakespeare quotations. When we're dead, no one will say things like 'Quis custodiet ipsos custodes?' anymore."

"And that'll be a loss, will it?"

"I can't tell if you're being ironic or not."

"Neither can I."

"Who was that British general in some Indian war who captured the province of Sind and sent a one-word telegram back to HQ? It simply said: 'Peccavi' . . . Ah, a few blank faces. Latin for 'I have sinned.'"

"Personally, I'm extremely glad those days are over."

"You'd probably prefer 'mission accomplished' or whatever they say."

"No, I just hate imperialist jokes about killing people."

"Pardon my Latin."

"Right. So moving swiftly back to Galileo. The earth going round the sun is something that's been proved as much as anything can be. But what about, say, climate change?"

"Well, we all believe in that, don't we?"

"Do you remember when Reagan said trees gave off carbon emissions, and people hung signs round the trunks of redwoods saying 'Sorry' and 'It's all my fault'?"

"Or, 'Peccavi.'"

"Indeed."

"But Reagan believed anything, didn't he? Like, he'd liberated some concentration camp in the war when all he'd done was stay in Hollywood and make patriotic films."

"Mind you, Bush made Reagan look good—almost classy."

"Someone said of Reagan that he was simple but not simpleminded."

"That's not bad."

"Yes, it is. It's sophistry, it's a spin doctor's formula. Hear it from me: simple is simpleminded."

"So we all believe in climate change?"

"Yes."

"Sure."

"But do we, for instance, believe that there's plenty of time for scientists to find a solution, or that we've reached a tipping point and in two, five or ten years it'll be too late, or that we've already passed that tipping point and we're going to hell in a handcart?"

"The middle one, don't we? That's why we all try to reduce our carbon footprint, and insulate our houses better, and recycle."

"Is recycling to do with global warming?"

"Need you ask?"

"Well, I only ask because we've been recycling for twenty years or so, and no one was talking about global warming back then."

"I sometimes think, when we're driving through central London in the evening and see all these office blocks with lights blazing away, that it's a bit bloody pointless worrying about leaving the telly and the computer on standby."

"Every little makes a difference."

"But every big makes a bigger difference."

"Did you see that terrifying statistic the other month—that something like seventy percent of passengers on flights in India were first-time fliers using budget airlines?"

"As they have every right to. We did. We still do, most of us, don't we?"

"Are you saying that out of some sense of fair play we have to let everyone else become as filthy and polluting and carbon-emitting as we've been, and only then do we have the moral right to suggest they stop it?"

"I'm not saying that. I'm saying they can hardly be expected to take lessons from us of all people."

"Do you know what I think is the most disgusting thing, morally, in the last twenty years or whatever. Emissions trading. Isn't that a disgusting idea?"

"All together now . . ."

"'It's the hypocrisy I can't stand.'"

"Beasts, all of you. But especially you, Dick."

"One thing really annoys me. You sort out all your recycling and put it in separate boxes, and then they come round with the van and throw it in higgledy-piggledy, mixing it all up again."

"But if we think we *are* at the tipping point, what chance do we believe we have of the world agreeing?"

"Perhaps as much as one chance in five?"

"Self-interest. That's what makes things tick. People will recognise it's in their own interest. And that of subsequent generations."

"Subsequent generations don't vote for today's politicians."

"What has posterity ever done for me, as someone asked."

"But politicians know that most *voters* care about subsequent generations. And most politicians are parents."

"I think one problem is that even if we accept self-interest as a useful guiding principle, there's a gap between what your actual self-interest is and what you perceive it to be."

"Also between short- and long-term self-interest."

"Wasn't it Keynes?"

"Wasn't what?"

"Said that thing about posterity."

"It's usually him or Oliver Wendell Holmes or Judge Learned Hand or Nubar Gulbenkian."

"I don't know who or what you're talking about."

"Did you see that French champagne houses are thinking of relocating to England because soon it'll be too warm for their grapes?"

"Well, in Roman times—"

"There were vineyards along Hadrian's Wall. You're always telling us that, Mr. Wine Bore."

"Am I? Well, it bloody bears repeating, because maybe it proves that it's just the great cycle of nature coming round again."

"The great recycle of nature."

"Except we know it isn't. Did you see that map of global warming in the paper the other day? It said a four-degree rise would be utterly disastrous—no water in most of Africa, cyclones, epidemics, rising sea levels, the Netherlands and southeast England underwater."

"Can't we rely on the Dutch to sort something out? They did before."

"What time span are we actually talking about?"

"If we don't agree now, we could have a four-degree rise by 2060."

"Ah."

"You know—I expect you'll all beat me up for this—but there are times when it feels almost glamorous to be part of the last generation."

"What last generation?"

"The last to use Latin tags. *Sunt lacrimae rerum.*"

"Well, looking at the human animal and its historical track record, it's perfectly possible we shan't get out of this one. So— the last generation to have been truly careless, truly without care."

"I don't know how you can say that. What about 9/11 and terrorism and AIDS and . . ."

"Swine flu."

"Yes, but they're all local, and in the long run minor."

"In the long run we are all dead—now that *was* Keynes."

"What about dirty bombs and nuclear war in the Middle East?"

"Local, local. What I was talking about was a sense that it's all out of control, all too late, nothing we can do about it . . ."

"Way past the tipping point . . ."

". . . and just as, in the past, people looked ahead and posited the rise of civilisation, the discovery of new continents, the understanding of the universe's secrets, now we are looking at a vista of grand reversal and inevitable, spectacular decline, when homo will become a lupus to homini again. As in the beginning, so it was in the end."

"Blimey, you *are* in apocalyptic mode."

"But you said glamorous. What's glamorous about the world burning up?"

"Because you, we, had the world before it did so, or before we realised that it would do so. We're like that generation which knew the world before 1914, only to the power of a thousand. From now on it's all about—what's that phrase?—managed decline."

"So you don't recycle?"

"Of course we do. I'm a good boy, like everyone else. But I quite see Nero's point. May as well fiddle while Rome burns."

"Do we believe he did? Isn't it like those famous sayings that nobody ever said?"

"Is it? Weren't there eyewitness accounts of Nero fiddling? Suetonius, as it were?"

"*Res ipsa loquitur.*"

"Tony, that's enough."

"I didn't know they had violins in Ancient Rome."

"Joanna, at last a pertinent observation."

"Isn't Stradivarius an old Roman name? Sounds like one."

"Isn't it amazing how much we don't know?"

"Or how much we know but how little we believe."

"Who was it said they had strong opinions weakly held?"

"Give up."

"I don't know either, I just remembered it."

"You know, our council has actually started to employ recycling snoopers. Can you imagine that?"

"Not until you tell us what they do."

"They come round looking at your recycling bins and check if you're recycling enough of something—"

"They actually come onto your property? I'd sue the buggers for trespass."

". . . and then if, say, they find you haven't put out enough tins, they'll shove a leaflet through the door explaining how to pull your socks up."

"Bloody cheek. Why not spend the money on extra nurses or something?"

"That's what it'll come to in apocalyptic Britain. Snoopers breaking down your front door to see if you've left your telly on standby."

"They wouldn't find many tins in our recycling, because we hardly buy any. Most of it's far too high in salt and preservatives and so on."

"Ah, but when the snoopers get to work on you, you'll be buying tins and chucking away the contents so you can keep up your recycling quota."

"Couldn't they replace snoopers with extra surveillance cameras?"

"Aren't we getting off the point?"

"What's new about that?"

"Stradivari."

"I beg your pardon."

"Stradivarius is the instrument, Stradivari the maker."

"Fine by me. Absolutely fine."

"When I was young, I used to hate the way the world was governed by old men, because they were obviously out of touch and mired in history. Now the politicians are all so bloody young they're out of touch in a different way, and I don't so much hate it as fear it, because they can't possibly understand enough about the world."

"When I was young, I liked short books. Now I'm older, and there's less time left, I find I prefer long books. Can anyone explain that?"

"Animal self-delusion. One part of you pretending that there's more time than there really is."

"When I was young and started listening to classical music, I used to prefer the fast movements and was bored by the slow movements. I just wanted them to be over. Now it's the opposite. I prefer slow movements."

"That's probably connected to the blood slowing down."

"Does the blood slow down? Just out of interest."

"If it doesn't, it ought to."

"Another thing we don't know."

"If it doesn't, it's still a metaphor and, as such, true."

"If only global warming were a metaphor."

"Slow movements are more moving. That's what it's about. The others have noise, excitement, initiation, conclusion. Slow movements are pure emotion. Elegiac, a sense of time passing, inevitable loss—that's slow movements for you."

"Does Phil know what he's talking about?"

"I always know what I'm talking about at this time of night."

"But why should we be more moved now? Are our emotions deeper?"

"Back then you were exhilarated and excited by the fast movements."

"Are you saying that the pool of emotions remains the same size, but pours out in different directions at different times?"

"I might be saying that."

"But surely we had our strongest emotions when we were young—falling in love, getting married, having children."

"But now perhaps we have longer emotions."

"Or our strongest emotions are of a different kind now—loss, regret, a sense of things ending."

"Don't be so gloomy. Wait till you have grandchildren. They'll surprise you."

"'All of the pleasure and none of the responsibility.'"

"Not that one again."

"I did put it in quotes."

"And a sense of life's continuance that I didn't get so much with my own children."

"That's because your grandchildren haven't disappointed you yet."

"Oh, don't say that."

"OK, I didn't say that."

"So do we think there's any hope for the planet? Given global warming, a failure to identify true self-interest, and the politicians being as young as policemen?"

"The human race has got itself out of scrapes before."

"And the young are more idealistic than we were. Or at least are."

"And Galileo is still winning against the pope. That's a kind of metaphor."

"And I still haven't got bum cancer. That's a kind of fact."

"Dick, something to finally tip the balance. The world is now a positive place to live in."

"We're all going to be just a bit warmer."

"And who'll miss the Netherlands? As long as they move the Rembrandts to higher ground."

"And a lot poorer because the bankers have stolen our money."

"And we'll all have to become vegetarians because meat production adds to global warming."

"And we shan't be able to travel as much, except on foot or on horse."

"'Shanks's pony'—people will start saying that again."

"You know, I've always envied those times when even people who could afford to travel abroad did so only once in their life-time. Not to mention the poor pilgrim with his stick and his scallop-shell badge making the one pilgrimage of his entire life."

"You're forgetting we're on the side of Galileo around this table."

"Then you can go on a pilgrimage to see his telescope in Flor-ence or wherever they keep it. Unless the pope burnt it."

"And we'll go back to growing more of our own food, which will be healthier."

"And repairing things like we used to."

"And making our own entertainment, and holding real con-versations over family meals, and showing proper respect to Grandma in the corner knitting socks for the new arrival and telling us tales of olden times."

"We don't want to go *that* far."

"Good, as long as we can still watch telly, and nuclear families are optional."

"What about using barter instead of money?"

"At least that would screw the bankers."

"Don't count on it. They'd soon find a way to make them-selves indispensable. There'll be a futures market in rainfall or sunshine or whatever."

"There already is, my friend."

"Remember how they used to say, 'The poor are always with us'?"

"So?"

"Well, it ought to have been 'The rich are always with us,' 'The bankers are always with us.'"

"I've just realised why it's called the nuclear family."

"Because it's fissile and always likely to explode and irradiate people."

"But I was going to say that."

"Too late."

"Hmm, the smell of that apple wood . . ."

"Question: which of our five senses could we most easily do without?"

"Too late for guessing games."

"We'll answer that next time."

"Talking of which . . ."

"Lovely food."

"That was the best."

"And no one mentioned the C-word."

"Or gave us sexual homework."

"Let me give you a toast instead."

"We don't do toasts around this table. House rules."

"It's all right, it isn't to anyone present. I just give you: the world in 2060. May they have as much pleasure as we do."

"The world in 2060."

"The world."

"Pleasure."

"Do you think people will still lie about sex in 2060?"

"Perhaps as many as one in five will."

"It was A. J. P. Taylor, by the way."

"Who was?"

"Who said he had strong opinions weakly held."

"Well, I raise a silent glass to him as well."

There was the usual shuffling, and putting on of coats, and hugging and kissing, and then we trooped out, heading down towards the minicab office and the Underground.

"Loved the smell of that fire," said Sue.

"And we didn't have to eat anything from a dead cow's mouth," said Tony.

"Odd to think we'll all be dead by 2060," said Dick.

"Oh, I wish you wouldn't say things like that," said Carol.

"Someone has to say the things other people don't," said David.

"I'll see you guys," said Larry. "I'm heading this way."

"See you," we mostly replied.

# Marriage Lines

THE TWIN OTTER was only half-full as they took off from Glasgow: a few islanders returning from the mainland, plus some early-season weekenders with hiking boots and rucksacks. For almost an hour they flew just above the shifting brainscape of the clouds. Then they descended, and the jigsaw edges of the island appeared below them.

He had always loved this moment. The neck of headland, the long Atlantic beach of Traigh Eais, the large white bungalow they ritually buzzed, then a slow turn over the little humpy island of Orosay, and a final approach to the flat, sheeny expanse of Traigh Mhòr. In summer months, you could usually count on some boisterous mainland voice, keen perhaps to impress a girlfriend, shouting over the propellor noise, "Only commercial beach landing in the world!" But with the years he had grown indulgent even about that. It was part of the folklore of coming here.

They landed hard on the cockle beach and spray flew up between the wing struts as they raced through shallow puddles. Then the plane slewed side on to the little terminal building, and a minute later they were climbing down the rickety metal steps to the beach. A tractor with a flatbed trailer was standing by to trundle their luggage the dozen yards to a damp concrete slab which served as the carousel. They, their: he knew he must start getting used to the singular pronoun instead. This was going to be the grammar of his life from now on.

Calum was waiting for him, looking past his shoulder, scanning the other passengers. The same slight, grey-haired figure in a green windcheater who met them every year. Being Calum, he didn't ask; he waited. They had known one another, with a kind of intimate formality, for twenty years or so. Now that regularity, that repetition, and all it contained, was broken.

As the van dawdled along the single-track road, and waited politely in the passing bays, he told Calum the story he was already weary with repeating. The sudden tiredness, the dizzy spells, the blood tests, the scans, hospital, more hospital, the hospice. The speed of it all, the process, the merciless tramp of events. He told it without tears, in a neutral voice, as if it might have happened to someone else. It was the only way, so far, that he knew how.

Outside the dark stone cottage, Calum yanked on the hand brake. "Rest her soul," he said quietly, and took charge of the holdall.


The first time they had come to the island, they weren't yet married. She had worn a wedding ring as a concession to . . . what?—their imagined version of island morality? It made them feel both superior and hypocritical at the same time. Their room at Calum and Flora's B & B had whitewashed walls, rain drying on the window, and a view across the machair to the sharp rise of Beinn Mhartainn. On their first night, they had discovered a bed whose joints wailed against any activity grosser than the minimum required for the sober conception of children. They found themselves comically restricted. Island sex, they had called it, giggling quietly into each other's bodies.

He had bought new binoculars especially for that trip. Inland, there were larks and twites, wheatears and wagtails. On the shoreline, ringed plovers and pipits. But it was the seabirds he loved best, the cormorants and gannets, the shags and fulmars. He spent many a docile, wet-bottomed hour on the clifftops, thumb and middle finger bringing into focus their whirling dives, and their soaring independence. The fulmars were his favourites. Birds which spent their whole lives at sea, coming to land only to nest. Then they laid a single egg, raised the chick, and took to the sea again, skimming the waves, rising on the air currents, being themselves.

She had preferred flowers to birds. Sea pinks, yellow rattle, purple vetch, flag iris. There was something, he remembered, called self-heal. That was as far as his knowledge, and memory, went. She had never picked a single flower here, or anywhere else. To cut a flower was to speed its death, she used to say. She hated the sight of a vase. In the hospital, other patients, seeing the empty metal trolley at the foot of her bed, had thought her friends neglectful, and tried to pass on their excess bouquets. This went on until she was moved to her own room, and then the problem ceased.

That first year, Calum had shown them the island. One afternoon, on a beach where he liked to dig for razor clams, he had looked away from them and said, almost as if he was addressing the sea, "My grandparents were married by declaration, you know. That was all you needed in the old days. Approval and declaration. You were married when the moon was waxing and the tide running—to bring you luck. And after the wedding there'd be a rough mattress on the floor of an outbuilding. For the first night. The idea was that you begin marriage in a state of humility."

"Oh, that's wonderful, Calum," she had said. But he felt it was a rebuke—to their English manners, their presumption, their silent lie.

The second year, they had returned a few weeks after getting married. They wanted to tell everyone they met; but here was one place they couldn't. Perhaps this had been good for them—to be silly with happiness and obliged into silence. Perhaps it had been their own way of beginning marriage in a state of humility.

He sensed, nevertheless, that Calum and Flora had guessed. No doubt it wasn't difficult, given their new clothes and their daft smiles. On the first night Calum gave them whisky from a bottle without a label. He had many such bottles. There was a lot more whisky drunk than sold on this island, that was for sure.

Flora had taken out of a drawer an old sweater which had belonged to her grandfather. She laid it on the kitchen table, ironing it with her palms. In the old days, she explained, the women of these islands used to tell stories with their knitting. The pattern of this jersey showed that her grandfather had come from Eriskay, while its details, its decorations, told of fishing and faith, of the sea and the sand. And this series of zigzags across the shoulder—*these here, look*—represented the ups and downs of marriage. They were, quite literally, marriage lines.

Zigzags. Like any newly married couple, they had exchanged a glance of sly confidence, sure that for them there would be no downs—or at least, not like those of their parents, or of friends already making the usual stupid, predictable mistakes. They would be different; they would be different from anyone who had ever got married before.

"Tell them about the buttons, Flora," said Calum.

The pattern of the jersey told you which island its owner came from; the buttons at the neck told you precisely which family they belonged to. It must have been like walking around dressed in your own postcode, he thought.

A day or two later, he had said to Calum, "I wish everyone was still wearing those sweaters." Having no sense of tradition himself, he liked other people to display one.

"They had great use," replied Calum. "There was many a drowning you could only recognise by the jersey. And then by the buttons. Who the man was."

"I hadn't thought of that."

"Well, no reason for it. For you to know. For you to think."

There were moments when he felt this was the most distant place he had ever come to. The islanders happened to speak the same language as him, but that was just some strange, geographical coincidence.

This time, Calum and Flora treated him as he knew they would: with a tact and modesty he had once, stupidly, Englishly, mistaken for deference. They didn't press themselves upon him, or make a show of their sympathy. There was a touch on the shoulder, a plate laid before him, a remark about the weather.

Each morning, Flora would give him a sandwich wrapped in greaseproof paper, a piece of cheese and an apple. He would set off across the machair and up Beinn Mhartainn. He made himself climb to the top, from where he could see the island and its jigsaw edges, where he could feel himself alone. Then, binoculars in hand, he would head for the cliffs and the seabirds. Calum had once told him that on some of the islands, generations back, they used to make oil for their lamps from the fulmars. Odd how he had always kept this detail from her, for twenty years and more. The rest of the year round, he never thought of it. Then they would come to the island, and he would say to himself, I mustn't tell her what they did with the fulmars.

That summer she had nearly left him (or had he nearly left her?—at this distance, it was hard to tell) he had gone clam digging with Calum. She had left them to pursue their sport, preferring to walk the damp, wavy line of the beach from which the sea had just retreated. Here, where the pebbles were barely bigger than sand grains, she liked to search for pieces of coloured glass—tiny shards of broken bottle, worn soft and smooth by water and time. For years he had watched the stooped walk, the inquisitive crouch, the picking, the discarding, the hoarding in the cupped left palm.

Calum explained how you looked for a small declivity in the sand, poured a little salt into it, then waited for the razor clam to shoot up a few inches from its lair. He wore an oven glove on his left hand, against the sharpness of the rising shell. You had to pull quickly, he said, seizing the clam before it disappeared again.

Mostly, despite Calum's expertise, nothing stirred, and they moved on to the next hollow in the sand. Out of the corner of his eye, he saw her wandering farther along the beach, her back turned to him, self-sufficient, content with what she was doing, not giving him a thought.

As he handed Calum more salt, and saw the oven glove poised in anticipation, he found himself saying, man to man, "Bit like marriage, isn't it?"

Calum frowned slightly. "What's your meaning?"

"Oh, waiting for something to pop out of the sand. Then it turns out either there's nothing there, or something that cuts your hand open if you aren't bloody careful."

It had been a stupid thing to say. Stupid because he hadn't really meant it, more stupid because it was presumptuous. Silence told him that Calum found such talk offensive, to himself, to Flora, to the islanders generally.

Each day he walked, and each day soft rain soaked into him. He ate a sodden sandwich, and watched the fulmars skimming the sea. He walked to Greian Head and looked down over the flat rocks where the seals liked to congregate. One year, they had watched a dog swim all the way out from the beach, chase the seals off, and then parade up and down its rock like a new landowner. This year there was no dog.

On the vertiginous flank of Greian was part of an unlikely golf course where, year after year, they had never seen a single golfer. There was a small circular green surrounded by a picket fence to keep the cows off. Once, nearby, a sudden herd of bullocks had rushed at them, frightening her silly. He had stood his ground, waved his arms wildly, instinctively shouted the names of the political leaders he most despised, and somehow not been surprised that it had calmed them down. This year, there were no bullocks to be seen, and he missed them. He supposed they must have long gone to slaughter.

He remembered a crofter on Vatersay telling them about lazy beds. You cut a slice of turf, placed your potatoes on the open soil, relaid the turf upside down on top of them—and that was it. Time and rain and the warmth of the sun did the rest. Lazy beds—he saw her laughing at him, reading his mind, saying afterwards that this would be his idea of gardening, wouldn't it? He remembered her eyes shining like the damp glass jewellery she used to fill her palm with.

On the last morning, Calum drove him back to Traigh Mhòr in the van. Politicians had been promising a new airstrip so that modern planes could land. There was talk of tourist development and island regeneration, mixed with warnings about the current cost of subsidy. Calum wanted none of it, and nor did he. He knew that he would need the island to stay as still and unchanging as possible. He wouldn't come back if jets started landing on tarmac.

He checked in his holdall at the counter, and they went outside. Hanging over a low wall, Calum lit a cigarette. They looked out across the damp and bumpy sand of the cockle beach. The cloud was low, the wind sock inert.

"These are for you," said Calum, handing him half a dozen postcards. He must have bought them at the café just now. Views of the island, the beach, the machair; one of the very plane waiting to take him away.

"But . . ."

"You will be needing the memory."

A few minutes later, the Twin Otter took off straight out across Orosay and the open sea. There was no farewell view of the island before that world below was shut out. In the enveloping cloud, he thought about marriage lines and buttons; about razor clams and island sex; about missing bullocks and fulmars being turned into oil; and then, finally, the tears came. Calum had known he would not be coming back. But the tears were not for that, or for himself, or even for her, for their memories. They were tears for his own stupidity. His presumption too.

He had thought he could recapture, and begin to say farewell. He had thought that grief might be assuaged, or if not assuaged, at least speeded up, hurried on its way a little, by going back to a place where they had been happy. But he was not in charge of grief. Grief was in charge of him. And in the months and years ahead, he expected grief to teach him many other things as well. This was just the first of them.

# Two

# The Limner

MR. TUTTLE had been argumentative from the beginning: about the fee—twelve dollars—the size of the canvas, and the prospect to be shown through the window. Fortunately, there had been swift accord about the pose and the costume. Over these, Wadsworth was happy to oblige the collector of customs; happy also to give him the appearance, as far as it was within his skill, of a gentleman. That was, after all, his business. He was a limner, but also an artisan, and paid at an artisan's rate to produce what suited the client. In thirty years, few would remember what the collector of customs had looked like; the only relic of his physical presence after he had met his Maker would be this portrait. And in Wadsworth's experience, clients held it more important to be pictured as sober, God-fearing men and women than they did to be offered a true likeness. This was not a matter that perturbed him.

From the edge of his eye, Wadsworth became aware that his client had spoken, but did not divert his gaze from the tip of his brush. Instead he pointed to the bound notebook in which so many sitters had written comments, expressed their praise and blame, wisdom and fatuity. He might as well open the book at any page and ask his client to identify a remark left by a predecessor ten or twenty years before. The opinions of this collector of customs so far had been as predictable as his waistcoat buttons, if less interesting. Fortunately, Wadsworth was paid to represent waistcoats rather than opinions. Of course, it was more complicated than this: to represent the waistcoat, and the wig, and the breeches, *was* to represent an opinion, indeed a whole corpus of them. The waistcoat and breeches showed the body beneath, as the wig and hat showed the brain beneath; though in some cases it was a pictorial exaggeration to suggest that any brains lay beneath.

He would be happy to leave this town, to pack his brushes and canvases, his pigments and palette, into the small cart, to saddle his mare and then take the forest trails which in three days would lead him home. There he would rest, and reflect, and perhaps decide to live differently, without this constant travail of the itinerant. A pedlar's life; also a supplicant's. As always, he had come to this town, taken lodgings by the night, and placed an advertisement in the newspaper, indicating his competence, his prices and his availability. "If no application is made within six days," the advertisement ended, "Mr. Wadsworth will quit the town." He had painted the small daughter of a dry-goods salesman, and then Deacon Zebediah Harries, who had given him Christian hospitality in his house, and recommended him to the collector of customs.

Mr. Tuttle had not offered lodging; but the limner willingly slept in the stable with his mare for company, and ate in the kitchen. And then there had been that incident on the third evening, against which he had failed—or felt unable—to protest. It had made him sleep uneasily. It had wounded him too, if the truth were known. He ought to have written the collector down for an oaf and a bully—he had painted enough in his years— and forgotten the matter. Perhaps he should indeed consider his retirement, let his mare grow fat, and live from what crops he could grow and what farmstock he could raise. He could always paint windows and doors for a trade instead of people; he would not judge this an indignity.

Late on the first morning, Wadsworth had been obliged to introduce the collector of customs to the notebook. The fellow, like many another, had imagined that merely opening his mouth wider might be enough to effect communication. Wadsworth had watched the pen travel across the page, and then the forefinger tap impatiently. "If God is merciful," the man wrote, "perhaps in Heaven you will hear." In reply, he had half smiled, and given a brief nod, from which surprise and gratitude might be inferred. He had read the thought many times before. Often it was a true expression of Christian feeling and sympathetic hope; occasionally, as now, it represented scarce-concealed dismay that the world contained those with such frustrating deformities. Mr. Tuttle was among those masters who preferred their servants to be mute, deaf and blind—except when his convenience suited the matter otherwise. Of course, masters and servants had become citizens and hired help once the juster republic had declared itself. But masters and servants did not thereby die out; nor did the essential inclinations of man.

Wadsworth did not think he was judging the collector in an un-Christian manner. His opinion had been forged on first contact, and confirmed on that third evening. The incident had been the crueller in that it involved a child, a garden boy who had scarcely entered the years of understanding. The limner always felt tenderly towards children: for themselves, for the grateful fact that they overlooked his deformity, and also because he had no issue himself. He had never known the company of a wife. Perhaps he might yet do so, though he would have to ensure that she was beyond childbearing years. He could not inflict his deformity on others. Some had tried explaining that his fears were unnecessary, since the affliction had arrived not at birth, but after an attack of the spotted fever when he was a boy of five.

Further, they pressed, had he not made his way in the world, and might not a son of his, howsoever constructed, do likewise? Perhaps that would be the case, but what of a daughter? The notion of a girl living as an outcast was too much for him. True, she might stay at home, and there would be a shared sympathy between them. But what would happen to such a child after his death?

No, he would go home and paint his mare. This had always been his intention, and perhaps now he would execute it. She had been his companion for twelve years, understood him easily, and took no heed of the noises that issued from his mouth when they were alone in the forest. His plan had been this: to paint her, on the same size of canvas used for Mr. Tuttle, though turned to make an oblong; and afterwards, to cast a blanket over the picture and uncover it only on the mare's death. It was presumptuous to compare the daily reality of God's living creation with a human simulacrum by an inadequate hand—even if this was the very purpose for which his clients employed him.

He did not expect it would be easy to paint the mare. She would lack the patience, and the vanity, to pose for him, with one hoof proudly advanced. But then, neither would his mare have the vanity to come round and examine the canvas even as he worked on it. The collector of customs was now doing so, leaning over his shoulder, peering and pointing. There was something he did not approve. Wadsworth glanced upwards, from the immobile face to the mobile one. Even though he had a distant memory of speaking and hearing, and had been taught his letters, he had never learnt the facility of reading words upon the tongue. Wadsworth raised the narrowest of his brushes from the waistcoat button's boss, and transferred his eye to the notebook as the collector dipped his pen. "More dignity," the man wrote, and then underlined the words.

Wadsworth felt that he had already given Mr. Tuttle dignity

enough. He had increased his height, reduced his belly, ignored the hairy moles on the fellow's neck, and generally attempted to represent surliness as diligence, irascibility as moral principle. And now he wanted more of it! This was an un-Christian demand, and it would be an un-Christian act on Wadsworth's part to accede to it. It would do the man no service in God's eyes if the limner allowed him to appear puffed up with all the dignity he demanded.

He had painted infants, children, men and women, and even corpses. Three times he had urged his mare to a deathbed where he was asked to perform resuscitation—to represent as living someone he had just met as dead. If he could do that, surely he should be able to render the quickness of his mare as she shook her tail against the flies, or impatiently raised her neck while he prepared the little painting cart, or pricked her ears as he made noises to the forest.

At one time he had tried to make himself understood to his fellow mortals by gesture and by sound. It was true that a few simple actions could be easily imitated: he could show, for example, how a client might wish to stand. But other gestures often resulted in humiliating games of guessing; while the sounds he was able to utter failed to establish either his requirements or his shared nature as a human being, part of the Almighty's work, if differently made. Women judged the noises he made embarrassing, children found them a source of benign interest, men a proof of imbecility. He had tried to advance in this way, but had not succeeded, and so he had retreated into the muteness they expected, and perhaps preferred. It was at this point that he purchased his calfskin notebook, in which all human statement and opinion recurred. "*Do you think, Sir, there will be painting in Heaven?*" "*Do you think, Sir, there will be hearing in Heaven?*"

But his understanding of men, such as it had developed, came less from what they wrote down, more from his mute observation. Men—and women too—imagined that they could alter their voice and meaning without it showing in their face. In this they were much deceived. His own face, as he observed the human carnival, was as inexpressive as his tongue; but his eye told him more than they could guess. Formerly, he had carried, inside his notebook, a set of handwritten cards, bearing useful responses, necessary suggestions, and civil corrections to what was being proposed. He even had one special card, for when he was being condescended to by his interlocutor beyond what he found proper. It read: "Sir, the understanding does not cease to function when the portals of the mind are blocked." This was sometimes accepted as a just rebuke, sometimes held to be an impertinence from a mere artisan who slept in the stable. Wadsworth had abandoned its use, not because of either such response, but because it admitted too much knowledge. Those in the world of tongue held all the advantages: they were his paymasters, they wielded authority, they entered society, they exchanged thoughts and opinions naturally. Though, for all this, Wadsworth did not see that speaking was in itself a promoter of virtue. His own advantages were only two: that he could represent on canvas those who spoke, and could silently observe their meaning. It would be foolish to give away this second advantage.

The business with the piano, for instance. Wadsworth had first enquired, by pointing to his fee scale, if the collector of customs wished for a portrait of the entire family, matching portraits of himself and his wife, or a joint portrait, with perhaps miniatures of the children. Mr. Tuttle, without looking at his wife, had pointed to his own breast, and written on the fee sheet, "Myself alone." Then he had glanced at his wife, put one hand to his chin, and added, "Beside the piano." Wadsworth had noticed the handsome rosewood instrument and asked with a gesture if he might go across to it. Whereupon he demonstrated several poses: from sitting informally beside the open keyboard with a favourite song on display, to standing more formally beside the instrument. Tuttle had taken Wadsworth's place, arranged himself, advanced one foot, and then, after consideration, closed the lid of the keyboard. Wadsworth deduced from this that only Mrs. Tuttle played the piano; further, that Tuttle's desire to include it was an indirect way of including her in the portrait. Indirect, and also less expensive.

The limner had shown the collector of customs some miniatures of children, hoping to change his mind, but Tuttle merely shook his head. Wadsworth was disappointed, partly for reasons of money, but more because his delight in painting children had increased as that in painting their progenitors had declined. Children were more mobile than adults, more deliquescent of shape, it was true. But they also looked him in the eye, and when you were deaf you heard with your eyes. Children held his gaze, and he thereby perceived their nature. Adults often looked away, whether from modesty or a desire for concealment; while some, like the collector, stared back challengingly, with a false honesty, as if to say, Of course my eyes are concealing things, but you lack the discernment to realise it. Such clients judged Wadsworth's affinity with children proof that he was as deficient in understanding as the children were. Whereas Wadsworth found in their affinity with him proof that they saw as clearly as he did.

When he had first taken up his trade, he had carried his brushes and pigments on his back, and walked the forest trails like a pedlar. He found himself on his own, reliant upon recommendation and advertisement. But he was industrious, and being possessed of a companionable nature, was grateful that his skill allowed him access to the lives of others. He would enter a household, and whether placed in the stable, quartered with the help, or, very occasionally, and only in the most Christian of dwellings, treated like a guest, he had, for those few days, a function and a recognition. This did not mean he was treated with any less condescension than other artisans; but at least he was being judged a normal human being, that is to say, one who merited condescension. He was happy, perhaps for the first time in his life.

And then, without any help beyond his own perceptions, he began to understand that he had more than just a function; he had strength of his own. This was not something those who employed him would admit; but his eyes told him that it was the case. Slowly he realised the truth of his craft: that the client was the master, except when he, James Wadsworth, was the client's master. For a start, he was the client's master when his eye discerned what the client would prefer him not to know. A husband's contempt. A wife's dissatisfaction. A deacon's hypocrisy. A child's suffering. A man's complacency at having his wife's money to spend. A husband's eye for the hired girl. Large matters in small kingdoms.

And beyond this, he realised that, when he rose in the stable and brushed the horsehair from his clothes, then crossed to the house and took up a brush made from the hair of another animal, he became more than he was taken for. Those who sat for him and paid him did not truly know what their money would buy. They knew what had been agreed—the size of the canvas, the pose and the decorative elements (the bowl of strawberries, the bird on a string, the piano, the view from a window)—and from this agreement they inferred mastery. But this was the very moment at which mastery passed to the other side of the canvas. Hitherto in their lives they had seen themselves in looking glasses and hand mirrors, in the backs of spoons, and, dimly, in clear still water. It was even said that lovers were able to see their reflections in each other's eyes; but the limner had no experience of this. Yet all such images depended upon the person in front of the glass, the spoon, the water, the eye. When Wadsworth provided his clients with their portraits, it was habitually the first time they had seen themselves as someone else saw them. Sometimes, when the picture was presented, the limner would detect a sudden chill passing over the subject's skin, as if he were thinking: so this is how I truly am? It was a moment of unaccountable seriousness: this image was how he would be remembered when he was dead. And then there was a seriousness beyond even this. Wadsworth did not think himself presumptuous when his eye told him that often the subject's next reflection was: and is this perhaps how the Almighty sees me too?

Those who did not have the modesty to be struck by such doubts tended to comport themselves as the collector now did: to ask for adjustments and improvements, to tell the limner that his hand and eye were faulty. Would they have the vanity to complain to God in His turn? "More dignity, more dignity." An instruction additionally repugnant given Mr. Tuttle's behaviour in the kitchen two nights ago.

Wadsworth had been taking his supper, content with his day's labour. He had just finished the piano. The instrument's narrow leg, which ran parallel to Tuttle's more massive limb, ended in a gilt claw, which Wadsworth had had some trouble in rendering. But now he was able to refresh himself, to stretch by the fire, to feed, and to observe the society of the help. There were more of these than expected. A collector of customs might earn fifteen dollars a week, enough to keep a hired girl. Yet Tuttle also kept a cook and a boy to work the garden. Since the collector did not appear to be a man lavish with his own money, Wadsworth deduced that it was Mrs. Tuttle's portion which permitted such luxury of attention.

Once they became accustomed to his deformity, the help treated him easily, as if his deafness rendered him their equal. It was an equality Wadsworth was happy to concede. The garden boy, an elf with eyes of burnt umber, had taken to amusing him with tricks. It was as if he imagined that the limner, being shorn of words, thereby lacked amusement. This was not the case, but he indulged this indulgence of him and smiled as the boy turned cartwheels, stole up behind the cook while she bent to the bake oven, or played a guessing game with acorns hidden in his fists.

The limner had finished his broth and was warming himself before the fire—an element Mr. Tuttle was not generous with elsewhere in the house—when an idea came to him. He drew a charred stick from the edge of the ashes, touched the garden boy on the shoulder to make him stay as he was, then pulled a drawing book from his pocket. The cook and the hired girl tried to watch what he was doing, but he held them away with a hand, as if to say that this particular trick, one he was offering in thanks for the boy's own tricks, would not work if observed. It was a rough sketch—it could only be so, given the crudeness of the implement—but it contained some part of a likeness. He tore the page from the book and handed it to the boy. The child looked up at him with astonishment and gratitude, placed the sketch on the table, took Wadsworth's drawing hand and kissed it. I should always paint children, the limner thought, looking the boy in the eye. He was almost unaware of the laughing tumult that broke out when the other two examined the drawing, and then of the silence which fell when the collector of customs, drawn by the sudden noise, entered the kitchen.

The limner watched as Tuttle stood there, one foot advanced, as in his portrait, his mouth opening and closing in a manner that did not suggest dignity. He watched as the cook and the girl rearranged themselves in more decorous attitudes. He watched as the boy, alert to his master's gaze, picked up the drawing and modestly, proudly, handed it over. He watched as Tuttle took the paper calmly, examined it, glanced at the boy, then at Wadsworth, nodded, deliberately tore the sketch in four, placed it in the fire, waited until it blazed, said something further when in quarter-profile to the limner, and made his exit. He watched as the boy wept.

The portrait was finished: both rosewood piano and collector of customs gleamed. The small white customs house filled the window at Mr. Tuttle's elbow—not that there was any real window there, nor, if there had been, any customs house visible through it. Yet everyone understood this modest transcendence of reality. And perhaps the collector, in his own mind, was only asking for a similar transcendence of reality when he demanded more dignity. He was still leaning over Wadsworth, gesturing at the representation of his face, chest, leg. It did not matter in the least that the limner could not hear what he was saying. He knew exactly what was meant, and also how little it signified. Indeed, it was an advantage not to hear, for the particularities would doubtless have raised him to an even greater anger than that which he presently felt.

He reached for his notebook. "Sir," he wrote, "we agreed upon five days for my labour. I must leave tomorrow morning by daybreak. We agreed that you would pay me tonight. Pay me, give me three candles, and by the morning I shall work such improvement as you require."

It was rare for him to treat a client with so little deference. It would be bad for his reputation in the county; but he no longer cared. He offered the pen in the direction of Mr. Tuttle, who did not deign to receive it. Instead, he left the room. While waiting, the limner examined his work. It was well done: the proportions pleasing, the colours harmonious, and the likeness within the bounds of honesty. The collector ought to be satisfied, posterity impressed, and his Maker—always assuming he was vouchsafed Heaven—not too rebuking.

Tuttle returned and handed over six dollars—half the fee—and two candles. Doubtless their cost would be deducted from the second half of the fee when it came to be paid. If it came to be paid. Wadsworth looked long at the portrait, which had come to assume for him equal reality with its fleshly subject, and then he made several decisions.

He took his supper as usual in the kitchen. His companions had been subdued the previous night. He did not think they blamed him for the incident with the garden boy; at most, they thought his presence had led to their own misjudgement, and so they were chastened. This, at any rate, was how Wadsworth saw matters, and he did not think their meaning would be clearer if he could hear speech or read lips; indeed, perhaps the opposite. If his notebook of men's thoughts and observations was anything to judge by, the world's knowledge of itself, when spoken and written down, did not amount to much.

This time, he selected a piece of charcoal more carefully, and with his pocketknife scraped its end to a semblance of sharpness. Then, as the boy sat opposite him, immobile more through apprehension than a sitter's sense of duty, the limner drew him again. When he had finished, he tore out the sheet and, with the boy's eyes upon him, mimed the act of concealing it beneath his shirt, and handed it across the table. The boy immediately did as he had seen, and smiled for the first time that evening. Next, sharpening his piece of charcoal before each task, Wadsworth drew the cook and the hired girl. Each took the sheet and concealed it without looking. Then he rose, shook their hands, embraced the garden boy, and returned to his night's work.

More dignity, he repeated to himself as he lit the candles and took up his brush. Well then, a dignified man is one whose appearance implies a lifetime of thought; one whose brow expresses it. Yes, there was an improvement to be made there. He measured the distance between the eyebrow and the hairline, and at the midpoint, in line with the right eyeball, he developed the brow: an enlargement, a small mound, almost as if something was beginning to grow. Then he did the same above the left eye. Yes, that was better. But dignity was also to be inferred from the state of a man's chin. Not that there was anything patently insufficient about Tuttle's jawline. But perhaps the discernible beginnings of a beard might help—a few touches on each point of the chin. Nothing to cause immediate remark, let alone offence, merely an indication.

And perhaps another indication was required. He followed the collector's sturdily dignified leg down its stockinged calf to the buckled shoe. Then he followed the parallel leg of the piano down from the closed keyboard lid to the gilt claw which had so delayed him. Perhaps that trouble could have been avoided? The collector had not specified that the piano be rendered exactly. If a little transcendence had been applied to the window and the customs house, why not to the piano as well? The more so, since the spectacle of a claw beside a customs man might suggest a grasping and rapacious nature, which no client would wish implied, whether there was evidence for it or no. Wadsworth therefore painted out the feline paw and replaced it with a quieter hoof, grey in colour and lightly bifurcated.

Habit and prudence urged him to snuff out the two candles he had been awarded; but the limner decided to leave them burning. They were his now—or at least, he would have paid for them soon. He washed his brushes in the kitchen, packed his painting box, saddled his mare and harnessed the little cart to her. She seemed as happy to leave as he. As they walked from the stable, he saw windows outlined by candlelight. He hauled himself into the saddle, the mare moved beneath him, and he began to feel cold air on his face. At daybreak, an hour from now, his penultimate portrait would be examined by the hired girl pinching out wasteful candles. He hoped that there would be painting in Heaven, but more than this he hoped that there would be deafness in Heaven. The mare, soon to be the subject of his final portrait, found her own way to the trail. After a while, with Mr. Tuttle's house now far behind them, Wadsworth shouted into the silence of the forest.

# Complicity

WHEN I WAS a hiccuping boy, my mother would fetch the back-door key, pull my collar away from my neck, and slip the cold metal down my back. At the time, I took this to be a normal medical—or maternal—procedure. Only later did I wonder if the cure worked merely by creating a diversion, or whether, perhaps, there was some more clinical explanation, whether one sense could directly affect another.

When I was a twenty-year-old, impossibly in love with a married woman who had no notion of my attachment and desire, I developed a skin condition whose name I no longer remember. My body turned scarlet from wrist to ankle, first itching beyond the power of calamine lotion, then lightly flaking, then fully peeling, until I had shed myself like some transmuting reptile. Bits of me fell into my shirt and trousers, into the bedclothes, onto the carpet. The only parts that didn't burn and peel were my face, my hands and feet, and my groin. I didn't ask the doctor why this was the case, and never told the woman of my love.

When I divorced, my doctor friend Ben made me show him my hands. I asked if modern medicine, as well as using leeches again, was also going back to palmistry; and if so, whether astrology and magnetism and the theory of humours could be far behind. He replied that he could tell from the colour of my hands and fingertips that I was drinking too much.

Later, wondering if I had been duped into cutting down, I asked him if he had been joking, or guessing. He turned my hands palm upwards, nodded in approval, and said he would now look out for unattached female medics who might not find me too repugnant.

The second time we met was at a party of Ben's; she had brought her mother. Have you watched mothers and daughters at parties together—and tried to work out who is taking care of whom? The daughter giving Mum a bit of an outing, the mum watching for the sort of men her daughter attracts? Or both at the same time. Even if they're playing best friends, there's often an extra flicker of formality added to the relationship. Disapproval either goes unexpressed, or is exaggerated, with a roll of the eye and a theatrical moue and a "She never takes any notice of me, anyway."

We were standing there, in a tight circle with a fourth person my memory has blanked. She was opposite me, and her mother on my left. I was trying to be myself, whatever that might be, and at the same time trying to make that self acceptable, if not actually pleasing. Pleasing to her mother, that is; I wasn't bold enough to try to please her directly—at least, not in company. I can't remember what we talked about, but it seemed to be going OK; perhaps the forgotten fourth helped. What I do remember was this: she had her right arm down by her side, and when she caught me looking in her general direction, she inconspicuously made the smoking gesture—you know, the first two fingers extended and slightly parted, the other fingers and thumb bent away out of sight. I thought: a doctor who smokes, that's a good sign. While the conversation continued, I got out my packet of Marlboro Lights, and without looking—my activity, too, was at waist level—extracted a single cigarette, returned the pack to my pocket, took the cigarette by the filter tip, passed it round her mother's back, felt it being taken from my fingers. Noting a slight pause on her part, I went back to my pocket, took out a book of matches, held it by the striking end, felt it being taken from my fingers, watched her light up, exhale, close the cover of the book matches, pass it back behind her mother. I received it, delicately, by the same end I had given it out.

I should add that it was perfectly obvious to her mother what we were doing. But she didn't say anything, sigh, give a prim glance, or rebuke me for being a drug peddler. I instantly liked her for this, assuming she approved of this complicity between me and her daughter. She could, I suppose, have been deliberately holding back her disapproval for strategic reasons. But I didn't care, or rather, didn't think to care, preferring to assume approval. Yet this isn't what I was trying to tell you. The point wasn't about her mum. The point was those three moments when an object had passed from one set of fingertips to another.

That was the nearest I got to her that evening, and for weeks to come.

Have you ever played that game where you sit in a circle and close your eyes, or are blindfolded, and have to guess what an object is just from the feel? And then you pass it on to the next person and they have to guess? Or, you keep your guesses to yourselves until you've all made up your minds, and then announce them at the same time?

Ben claims that once, when he played it, a mozzarella cheese was passed round and three people guessed it was a breast implant. That may just be medical students for you; but there's something about closing your eyes which makes you more vulnerable, or drives the imagination to the gothic—especially if the object being passed is soft and squishy. In the times I played the game the most successful mystery item, the one guaranteed to freak somebody out, was a peeled lychee.

There was a production of *King Lear* I went to some years ago—

ten, fifteen?—played against a bare-brick backdrop, with brutal-
istic staging. I can't remember who directed it, or who played the
title role; though I do remember the blinding of Gloucester. This
is usually done with the earl pinioned and bent back over a chair.
Cornwall says to his servants, "Fellows, hold the chair," and then
to Gloucester, "Upon these eyes of thine I'll set my foot." One eye
is put out, and Regan chillingly comments, "One side will mock
another; the other too." Then, a moment later, the famous "Out,
vile jelly," and Gloucester is pulled upright, with stage gore drip-
ping down his face.

In the production I saw, the blinding was done offstage. I
seem to remember Gloucester's legs flailing from one of the
brick wings, though perhaps that is a later invention. But I do remember his screams, and finding them the more terrifying for
being offstage: perhaps what you can't see frightens you more
than what you can. And then, after the first eye was put out, it
was lobbed onto the stage. In my memory—in my mind's eye—I
see it rolling down the rake, faintly glistening. More screams, and
another eye was tossed out from the wings.

They were—you guessed—peeled lychees. And then this
happened: Cornwall, lanky and brutish, stamped back onstage,
tracked down the rolling lychees, and set his foot on Gloucester's
eyes a second time.

Another game, from back when I was a hiccuping boy at primary
school. In the morning break we used to race model cars in the
asphalt playground. They were about four inches long, made
from cast metal, and had real rubber tyres which you could roll
off the wheels if you felt like simulating a pit stop. They were
painted in the bright colours worn by the racing marques of
the day: a scarlet Maserati, a green Vanwall, a blue . . . perhaps
something French.

The game was simple: the car that went the farthest won. You pressed your thumb down onto the middle of the long bonnet, pulling your fingers up into a loose fist, and then, at a signal, transferred the pressure swiftly from a downwards to a forwards direction, sending your car off into the distance. There was a certain technique involved in obtaining maximum propulsion, the danger being that the knuckle of your middle finger, held a fraction of an inch above the playground's surface, would scrape against the asphalt, tearing skin and costing you the race. The wound would scab up, and you would have to adjust your hand, dropping the knuckle of the third finger into the danger area. But this could never produce the same velocity, so you went back to the usual, middle-finger technique, often ripping off the newly formed scab.

Your parents never warn you about the right things, do they? Or perhaps they can only warn you about the immediate, local stuff. They bandage the knuckle of your right middle finger and warn against getting it infected. They explain about the dentist, and how the pain will wear off afterwards. They teach you the highway code—or at least, as it applies to junior pedestrians. My brother and I were once about to cross a road when our father put on a firm voice and instructed us to "Pause on the kerb." We were at that age when a primitive understanding of language is intersected by a kind of giddiness about its possibilities. We looked at one another, shouted, "Paws on the kerb," then squatted down with our hands flat on the edge of the roadway. Our father thought this was very silly; no doubt he was already calculating how long the joke would run.

Nature warned us, our parents warned us. We understood about knuckle-scabbing and traffic. We learnt to look out for a loose stair carpet, because Grandma had once nearly taken a tumble when one of her brass stair rods, removed for annual polishing, hadn't been replaced properly. We learnt about thin ice, and frostbite, and evil boys who put pebbles and sometimes even razor blades into snowballs—though none of these warnings was ever justified by events. We learnt about nettles and thistles, and how grass, which seemed such harmless stuff, could give you a sudden burn, like sandpaper. We were warned about knives and scissors and the danger of the untied shoelace. We were warned about strange men who might try to lure us into cars or lorries; though it took us years to work out that "strange" did not mean "bizarre, hunchbacked, dribbling, goitred"—or however we defined strangeness—but merely "unknown to us." We were warned about bad boys and, later, bad girls. An embarrassed science master warned us against VD, misleadingly informing us that it was caused by "indiscriminate sexual intercourse." We were warned about gluttony and sloth and letting down our school, about avarice and greed and letting down our family, about envy and wrath and letting down our country.

We were never warned about heartbreak.


I used the word "complicity" a bit ago. I like the word. An unspoken understanding between two people, a kind of presense if you like. The first hint that you may be suited, before the nervous trudgery of finding out whether you "share the same interests," or have the same metabolism, or are sexually compatible, or both want children, or however it is that we argue consciously about our unconscious decisions. Later, when we look back, we will fetishise and celebrate the first date, the first kiss, the first holiday together, but what really counts is what happened before this public story: that moment, more of pulse than of thought, which goes, Yes, perhaps her, and, Yes, perhaps him.

I tried to explain this to Ben, a few days after his party. Ben is a crossword-doer, a dictionary-lover, a pedant. He told me that "complicity" means a shared involvement in a crime or sin or nefarious act. It means planning to do something bad.

I prefer to keep the term as I understand it. For me it means planning to do something good. She and I were both free adults, capable of making our own decisions. And nobody plans to do anything bad at that moment, do they?

We went to a film together. I had as yet no clear sense of her temperament and habits. Whether she was punctual or unpunctual, easygoing or quick-tempered, tolerant or severe, cheerful or depressive, sane or mad. That may sound a crude way of putting it; besides, understanding another human being is hardly a matter of box-ticking in which the answers stay the answers. It's perfectly possible to be cheerful *and* depressive, easygoing *and* quick-tempered. What I mean is, I was still working out the default setting of her character.

It was a cold December afternoon; we arrived at the cinema in separate cars, as she was on call and might be bleeped back into the hospital. I sat there, watching the film, yet equally alert to her reactions: a smile, silence, tears, a shrinking from violence—all would be like silent bleeps for my information. The heating in the cinema was underpowered, and as we sat there, elbow to elbow on the armrest, I found myself thinking outwards from me to her. Sleeve of shirt, sweater, jacket, raincoat, pea jacket, jumper—and then what? Nothing more before flesh? So, six layers between us, or perhaps seven if she was wearing something with sleeves under her sweater.

The film passed; her mobile didn't pulse; I liked the way she laughed. It was already dark when we got outside. We had walked halfway to our cars when she stopped and held up her left hand, palm towards me.

"Look," she said.

I didn't know what I was meant to be looking for: proof of alcoholism, her line of life? I moved closer, and noticed, with the occasional help of passing headlights, that the tips of her first, second and third fingers had turned a pale yellowish colour.

"Twenty yards without gloves," she said. "It happens just like that." She told me the name of the syndrome. It was a question of poor circulation, of the cold making the blood concentrate in more important areas and withdraw from the extremities.

She found her gloves: dark brown ones, I remember. She pulled them on a little haphazardly, then meshed her fingers to push the wool down to the base of each finger. We walked on, discussing the film, paused, smiled, paused, parted; my car was parked ten yards beyond hers. As I was about to unlock it, I glanced back. She was still standing on the pavement, looking down. I gave her a few moments, decided something was wrong, and walked back.

"The car keys," she said without looking up at me. There wasn't much light and she was digging in her bag, feeling as much as looking for them. Then she added, with sudden violence, "Come on, you fool."

For a moment I thought she was talking to me. Then I realised she was angry only with herself, embarrassed by herself, and the more embarrassed that her inability to find her keys—and also, perhaps, her anger—were being witnessed by me. But I was hardly going to dock her points. As I stood there, watching her struggle, two things happened: I felt what I would describe as tenderness, were it not so ferocious; and my cock gave a sudden spurt of growth.

I remembered the first time a dentist gave me an injection; he left the room while the anaesthetic took effect, returned briskly, slid his finger into my mouth, ran it round the base of the tooth he was going to fill, and asked if I felt anything. I remembered the numbness that strikes when you sit too long with your legs crossed. I remembered stories of doctors pushing pins into a patient's leg without the patient reacting at all.

What I wanted to know the answer to was this. If I had been bolder, if I had raised my right hand against her left, laid palm gently against palm, finger against finger, in some lovers' high five, and if I had then pressed the tips of my first, second and third fingers against hers, would she have felt anything? What does it feel like when there's no feeling there—both to her, and to me? She sees my fingers against hers, but feels nothing; I see my fingers against hers, and feel them, but know that she feels nothing?

And of course I was also asking myself the question in a wider, more alarming sense.

I thought about one person wearing gloves and the other one not; about how flesh feels against wool, wool against flesh.

I tried to imagine all the gloves she might wear, both now and in the future—if there was to be a future I was present in.

I'd seen one pair of brown woollen gloves. I decided, given her condition, to equip her with several extra pairs in different colours. Then, for colder days and nights, some warmer, suede ones: black, I imagined (to match her hair), with heavy white stitching along the fingers, and beigey rabbit-fur lining. And then perhaps a pair of those gloves like paws, with a single thumb and a broad pouch for the fingers.

At work she would presumably wear surgical gloves, thin, latex ones offering the least barrier between doctor and patient— and yet any barrier destroys that essential feel of flesh on flesh. Surgeons wear tight-fitting gloves, other medical staff looser ones, like those you see in delis when you order ham, and watch slices peeled from the rotating blade.

I wondered if she was, or would ever become, a gardener.

She might wear latex gloves for light work in well-tilled soil, for sorting out rootlets and seedlings and delicate foliage. But then she would need a stronger pair—I imagined yellow cotton backs, with grey leather palms and fingers—for heavier work: pruning, forking the ground over, pulling up bindweed and nettle roots.

I wondered if she had any use for mitts. I've never seen the point of them myself. Who wears them, apart from Russian sleigh-drivers and misers in TV Dickens? And given what happened to the tips of her fingers, all the more reason not to.

I wondered if the circulation to her feet was curtailed as well, in which case: bed socks. What would they be like? Big and woolly—perhaps some ex-boyfriend's rugby socks, which would fall loosely around her ankles when she stood up? Or close-fitting and female? In some lifestyle supplement, I'd seen gaudy bed socks made with individual toes. I wondered if I'd find them a neutral accessory, comic, or somehow erotic.

What else? Might she ski, and have a pair of puffy gloves to match a puffy jacket? Oh, and of course, washing-up gloves: all women had them. And always in the same, brashly unconvincing colours—yellow, pink, pale green, pale blue. You'd have to be a pervert to find washing-up gloves erotic. Make them as exotic as you like—magenta, ultramarine, teak, pinstripe, Prince of Wales check—they'd never do anything for me.


No one says, "Feel this piece of Parmesan," do they? Except perhaps Parmesan makers.

Sometimes, alone in a lift, I will run my fingers lightly over the buttons. Not enough to change the floor I'm going to, just to feel the bumpy dots of Braille. And to wonder what it must be like.

The first time I saw someone wearing a thumbstall, I couldn't believe that there was a real thumb underneath it.

Do the slightest damage to the least important finger, and the whole hand is affected. Even the simplest actions—pulling on a sock, doing up a button, changing gear—become fraught, self-conscious. The hand won't go into a glove, has to be thought about when washed, mustn't be lain on at night, and so on.

Imagine, then, trying to make love with a broken arm.

I had a sudden, acute desire that nothing bad ever happen to her.

I once saw a man on a train. I was eleven or twelve, alone in my compartment. He came down the corridor, looked in, saw it was occupied, and passed on. I noticed that the arm he carried by his side ended in a hook. At the time, I thought only of pirates and menace; later, of all you couldn't do; later still, of the phantom pain of amputees.

Our fingers must work together; our senses too. They act for themselves, but also as pre-senses for the others. We feel a fruit for ripeness; we press our fingers into a joint of meat to test for doneness. Our senses work together for the greater good: they are complicit, as I like to say.

Her hair was up that evening, held by a pair of tortoiseshell combs, then pinned with gold. It was not quite as black as her eyes, but blacker than her linen jacket, which had a fade and a crease to it. We were in a Chinese restaurant and the waiters were paying proper attention to her. Perhaps her hair looked a bit Chinese; or perhaps they knew it was more important to please her than me—that pleasing her *was* pleasing me. She asked me to order, and I chose conservatively. Seaweed, spring rolls, green beans in yellow-bean sauce, crispy fried duck, stewed aubergine, plain boiled rice. A bottle of Gewürztraminer and tap water.

My senses were more alert than usual that evening. As I'd followed her from the car, I noticed her lightly floral scent; but this was soon blotted out by restaurant smells, as a mound of glistening spare ribs passed our table. And when the food came, it was the familiar amicable contest of taste and texture. The paperiness of the chopped leaf they call seaweed; the crunch of the beans in the heat of their sauce; the slick of plum sauce with the bite of spring onion and the firm shred of duck, all wrapped in the parchment pancake.

The background music offered a milder contrast of textures: from easy-listening Chinese to unobtrusive Western. Mostly ignorable, except when some overfamiliar film number nagged away. I suggested that if "Lara's Theme" from *Doctor Zhivago* came up, we should both make a run for it and plead duress in court. She asked if duress was really a defence in law. I went on at what might have been too great a length about this, then we talked about where our professional areas overlapped: where law came into medicine, and medicine into law. This led us on to smoking, and at which precise point we'd like to light up if it wasn't now banned. After the main course and before the pudding, we agreed. We each declared ourselves light smokers, and each half believed the other. Then we talked a little, but warily, about our childhoods. I asked how old she had been when she first noticed the ends of her fingers turning yellow in the cold, and whether she had many pairs of gloves, which made her laugh for some reason. Perhaps I'd hit upon one of the truths of her wardrobe. I almost asked her to describe her favourite gloves, but thought she might get the wrong idea.

And as the meal went on, I decided that it was going to be all right—though by "it" I meant only the evening; I could see no farther. And she must have felt the same, because when the waiter asked about pudding she didn't look at her watch apologetically, but said she could just find room for something as long as it wasn't sticky and filling, so chose the lychees. And I decided not to tell her about that game from long ago, nor about that production of *King Lear*. And then I did momentarily dare a future, and thought that if we came back again sometime, maybe I'd tell her. I also hoped that she'd never played the game with Ben, and been handed a mozzarella.

Just as I was thinking this, "Lara's Theme" oozed out of the speakers. We looked at one another and laughed, and she made a gesture as if to push back her chair and rise. Maybe she saw alarm in my eyes because she laughed again and then, playing along, threw her napkin down on the table. The gesture took her hand more than halfway across the cloth. But she didn't get up, or push her chair back, just went on smiling, and left her hand on top of her napkin, knuckles raised.

And then I touched her.

# Harmony

THEY HAD DINED well at 261 Land-strasse, and now passed eagerly into the music room. M——'s intimates had sometimes been fortunate enough to have Gluck, Haydn or the young prodigy Mozart perform for them; but they could be equally content when their host seated himself behind his violoncello and beckoned at one of them to accompany him. This time, however, the lid of the klavier was down, and the violoncello nowhere visible. Instead, they were confronted by an oblong rosewood box standing on legs which made the shape of matching lyres; there was a wheel at one end and a treadle beneath. M—— folded back the curved roof of the contraption, disclosing three dozen glass hemispheres linked by a central spindle and half submerged in a trough of water. He seated himself at the centre and pulled out a narrow drawer on either side of him. One contained a shallow bowl of water, the other a plate bearing fine chalk.

"If I might make a suggestion," said M——, looking round at his guests. "Those of you who have not yet heard Miss Davies's instrument might try the experiment of closing your eyes." He was a tall, well-made man in a blue frock coat with flat brass buttons; his features, strong and jowly, were those of a stolid Swabian, and if his bearing and voice had not obviously denoted the gentry, he might have been taken for a prosperous farmer. But it was his manner, courteous yet persuasive, which impelled some who had already heard him play decide to close their eyes as well.

M—— soaked his fingertips in water, flicked them dry and dabbled them in the chalk. As he pumped at the treadle with his right foot, the spindle turned on its bright brass gudgeons. He touched his fingers to the revolving glasses, and a high, lilting sound began to emerge. It was known that the instrument had cost fifty gold ducats, and sceptics among the audience at first wondered why their host had paid so much to reproduce the keening of an amorous cat. But as they became accustomed to the sound, they started to change their minds. A clear melody was becoming detectable: perhaps something of M——'s own composition, perhaps a friendly tribute to, or even theft from, Gluck. They had never heard such music before, and the fact that they were blind to the method by which it came to them emphasised its strangeness. They had not been told what to expect and so, guided only by their reasoning and sentiment, wondered if such unearthly noises were not precisely that— unearthly.

When M—— paused for a few moments, busying himself on the hemispherical glasses with a small sponge, one of the guests, without opening his eyes, observed, "It is the music of the spheres."

M—— smiled. "Music seeks harmony," he replied, "just as the human body seeks harmony." This was, and at the same time was not, an answer; rather than lead, he preferred to let others, in his presence, find their own way. The music of the spheres was heard when all the planets moved through the heavens in concert. The music of the earth was heard when all the instruments of an orchestra played together. The music of the human body was heard when it too was in a state of harmony, the organs at peace, the blood flowing freely and the nerves aligned along their true and intended paths.

The encounter between M—— and Maria Theresia von P—— took place in the imperial city of V—— between the winter of 177– and the summer of the following year. Such minor suppressions of detail would have been a routine literary mannerism at the time; but they also tactfully admit the partiality of our knowledge. Any philosopher claiming that his field of understanding was complete, and that a final, harmonious synthesis of truth was being offered to the reader, would have been denounced as a charlatan; and likewise those philosophers of the human heart who deal in storytelling would have been—and would be—wise not to make any such claim either.

We can know, for instance, that M—— and Maria Theresia von P—— had met before, a dozen years previously; but we cannot know whether or not she had any memory of the event. We can know that she was the daughter of Rosalia Maria von P——, herself the daughter of Thomas Cajetan Levassori della Motta, dance master at the imperial court; and that Rosalia Maria had married the imperial secretary and court counsellor Joseph Anton von P—— at the Stefanskirche on 9 November 175–. But we cannot tell what the mixing of such different bloods entailed, and whether it was in some way the cause of the catastrophe that befell Maria Theresia.

Again, we know that she was baptised on 15 May 175–, and that she learnt to place her fingers on a keyboard almost as soon as she learnt to place her feet on the floor. The child's health was normal, according to her father's account, until the morning of 9 December 176–, when she woke up blind; she was then three and a half years old. It was held to be a perfect case of amaurosis: that is to say, there was no fault detectable in the organ itself, but the loss of sight was total. Those summoned to examine her attributed the cause to a fluid with repercussions, or else to some fright the girl had received during the night. Neither parents nor servants, however, could attest to any such happening.

Since the child was both cherished and wellborn, she was not neglected. Her musical talent was encouraged, and she attracted both the attention and the patronage of the empress herself. A pension of two hundred gold ducats was granted to the parents of Maria Theresia von P——, with her education separately accounted for. She learnt the harpsichord and pianoforte with Kozeluch, and singing under Righini. At the age of fourteen she commissioned an organ concerto from Salieri; by sixteen she was an adornment of both salons and concert societies.

To some who gawped at the imperial secretary's daughter while she played, her blindness enhanced her appeal. But the girl's parents did not want her treated as the society equivalent of a fairground novelty. From the start, they had continually sought her cure. Professor Stoerk, court physician and head of the Medical Faculty, was regularly in attendance, and Professor Barth, celebrated for his operations on cataract, was also consulted. A succession of cures was tried, but as each failed to alleviate the girl's condition, she became prone to irritation and melancholia, and was assailed by fits which caused her eyeballs to bulge from their sockets. It might have been predictable that the confluence of music and medicine brought about the second encounter between M—— and Maria Theresia.


M—— was born at Iznang on Lake Constance in 173–. The son of an episcopal gamekeeper, he studied divinity at Dillingen and Ingolstadt, then took a doctorate in philosophy. He arrived in V—— and became a doctor of law before turning his attention to medicine. Such an intellectual peripeteia did not, however, indicate inconstancy, still less the soul of a dilettante. Rather M—— sought, like Doctor Faustus, to master all forms of human knowledge; and like many before him his eventual purpose—or dream—was to find a universal key, one that would permit the final understanding of what linked the heavens to the earth, the spirit to the body, all things to one another.

In the summer of 177–, a distinguished foreigner and his wife were visiting the imperial city. The lady was taken ill, and her husband—as if such were a normal medical procedure— instructed Maximilian Hell, astronomer (and member of the Society of Jesus), to prepare a magnet which might be applied to the afflicted part. Hell, a friend of M——'s, kept him informed of the commission; and when the lady's ailment was said to be cured, M—— hastened to her bedside to inform himself about the procedure. Shortly thereafter, he began his own experiments. He ordered the construction of numerous magnets of different sizes: some to be applied to the stomach, others to the heart, still others to the throat. To his own astonishment, and the gratitude of his patients, M—— discovered that cures beyond the prowess of a physician could sometimes be effected; the cases of Fräulein Oesterlin and the mathematician Professor Bauer were especially noted.

Had M—— been a fairground quack, and his patients cred- ulous peasants crowded into some rank booth, as eager to be relieved of their savings as of their pain, society would have paid no attention. But M—— was a man of science, of wide curiosity, and not obvious immodesty, who made no claims beyond what he could account for.

"It works," Professor Bauer had commented, as his breath came more easily and he was able to raise his arms beyond the horizontal. "But how does it work?"

"I do not yet understand it," M—— had replied. "When mag- nets were employed in past ages, it was explained that they drew illness to them just as they attracted iron filings. But we cannot sustain such an argument nowadays. We are not living in the age of Paracelsus. Reason guides our thinking, and reason must be applied, the more so when we are dealing with phenomena which lurk beneath the skin of things."

"As long as you do not propose to dissect me in order to find out," replied Professor Bauer.

In those early months, the magnetic cure was as much a matter of scientific enquiry as of medical practice. M—— experimented with the positioning of the magnets and the number applied to the patient. He himself often wore a magnet in a leather bag around his neck to increase his influence, and used a stick, or wand, to indicate the course of realignment he was seeking in the nerves, the blood, the organs. He magnetised pools of water and had patients place their hands, their feet, and sometimes their whole bodies in the liquid. He magnetised the cups and glasses they drank from. He magnetised their clothes, their bed-sheets, their looking glasses. He magnetised musical instruments so that a double harmony might result from their playing. He magnetised cats, dogs and trees. He constructed a *baquet*, an oaken tub containing two rows of bottles filled with magnetised water. Steel rods emerging from holes in the lid were placed against afflicted parts of the body. Patients were sometimes encouraged to join hands and form a circle round the *baquet*, since M—— surmised that the magnetic stream might augment in force as it passed through several bodies simultaneously.

"Of course I remember the *gnädige Fräulein* from my days as a medical student, when I was sometimes permitted to accompany Professor Stoerk." Now M—— was himself a member of the Faculty, and the girl was almost a woman: plump, with a mouth that turned down and a nose that turned up. "And though I can recall the description of her condition then, I would nonetheless like to ask questions which I fear you have answered many times already."

"Of course."

"There is no possibility that the Fräulein was blind from birth?"

M—— noticed the mother impatient to reply, but restraining herself.

"None," her husband said. "She saw as clearly as her brothers and sisters."

"And she was not ill before becoming blind?"

"No, she was always healthy."

"And did she receive any kind of shock at the time of her misfortune, or shortly before?"

"No. That is to say, none that we or anyone else observed."

"And afterwards?"

This time the mother did answer. "Her life has always been as protected against shock as we are able to make it. I would tear out my own eyes if I thought it would give Maria Theresia back her sight."

M—— was looking at the girl, who did not react. It was probable that she had heard this unlikely solution before.

"So her condition has been constant?"

"Her blindness has been constant"—the father again—"but there are periods when her eyes twitch convulsively and without cease. And her eyeballs, as you may see, are extruded, as if trying to escape their sockets."

"You are aware of such periods, Fräulein?"

"Of course. It feels as if water is slowly rushing in to fill my head, as if I shall faint."

"And she suffers in the liver and the spleen afterwards. They become disorderly."

M—— nodded. He would need to be present at such an

attack in order to guess its causes and observe its progress. He wondered how that might best be effected.

"May I ask the doctor a question?" Maria Theresia had lifted her head slightly towards her parents.

"Of course, my child."

"Does your procedure cause pain?"

"None that I inflict myself. Though it is often the case that patients need to be brought to a certain . . . pitch before harmony can be restored."

"I mean, do your magnets cause electric shocks?"

"No, that I may promise you."

"But if you do not cause pain, then how can you cure? Everyone knows that you cannot remove a tooth without pain, you cannot set a limb without pain, you cannot cure insanity without pain. A doctor causes pain, that the world knows. And that I know too."

Since she had been a small child the finest doctors had employed the most respected methods. There had been blistering and cauterising and the application of leeches. For two months her head had been encased in a plaster designed to provoke suppuration and draw the poison from her eyes. She had been given countless purges and diuretics. Most recently, electricity had been resorted to, and over the twelvemonth some three thousand electric shocks had been administered to her eyes, sometimes as many as a hundred in a single treatment.

"You are quite sure that magnetism will not cause me pain?"

"Quite sure."

"Then how can it possibly cure me?"

M—— was pleased to glimpse the brain behind the unseeing eyes. A passive patient, merely waiting to be acted upon by an omnipotent physician, was a tedious thing; he preferred those like this young woman, who displayed forcefulness beneath her good manners.

"Let me put it this way. Since you went blind, you have endured much pain at the hands of the best doctors in the city?"

"Yes."

"And yet you are not cured?"

"No."

"Then perhaps pain is not the only gateway to cure."

In the two years he had practised magnetic healing, M—— had constantly pondered the question of how and why it might work. A decade previously, in his doctoral thesis *De planetarum influxu*, he had proposed that the planets influenced human actions and the human body through the medium of some invisible gas or liquid, in which all bodies were immersed, and which for want of a better term he called "*gravitas universalis*." Occasionally, man might glimpse the overarching connection, and feel able to grasp the universal harmony that lay beyond all local discordance. In the present instance, magnetic iron arrived on earth in the form and body of a meteor fallen from the heavens. Once here, it displayed its singular property, the power to realign. Might one not surmise, therefore, that magnetism was the great universal force which bound together stellar harmony? And if so, was it not reasonable to expect that in the sublunary world it had the power to placate certain corporeal disharmonies?

It was evident, of course, that magnetism could not cure every bodily failing. It had proved most successful in cases of stomach-ache, gout, insomnia, ear trouble, liver and menstrual disorder, spasm, and even paralysis. It could not heal a broken bone, cure imbecility or syphilis. But in matters of nervous complaint, it might often effect startling improvement. Again, it could not overcome a patient mired in scepticism and disbelief, or one whose pessimism or melancholy undermined the possibility of a return to health. There must be a willingness to admit and welcome the effects of the procedure.

To this end, M—— sought to create, in his consulting room at 261 Landstrasse, an atmosphere sympathetic to such acceptance. Heavy curtains were drawn against the sun and external noise; his staff were forbidden from making sudden movements; there was calm and candlelight. Gentle music might be heard from another room; sometimes M—— would himself play upon Miss Davies's glass armonica, reminding both bodies and minds of the universal harmony that he was, in this small part of the world, seeking to restore.

M—— commenced his treatment on 20 January 177–. An external examination confirmed that Maria Theresia's eyes showed severe malformation: they were quite out of their normal alignment, grossly swollen and extruded. Internally, the girl seemed to be at a pitch where the passing phases of hysteria might lead to chronic derangement. Given that she had suffered fourteen years of disappointed hope, and fourteen years of unremitting blindness, this was not an unreasonable response from a young body and mind. M—— therefore began by emphasising again how different his procedure was from all others; how it was not a matter of order being reimposed by external violence, but rather of a collaboration between doctor and patient, aimed at reestablishing the natural alignment of the body. M—— talked generally; in his experience it did not help for the patient to be constantly aware of what was to be expected. He did not speak of the crisis he hoped to provoke, or predict the extent of the cure he envisioned. Even to the girl's parents, he expressed only the humble ambition of alleviating the gross ocular extrusion.

He explained his initial actions carefully, so they would come as no surprise. Then he addressed the loci of sensitivity on Maria Theresia's head. He placed his hands, formed into cups, around her ears; he stroked her skull from the base of the neck to the forehead; he placed his thumbs on her cheeks, just below the eyes, and made circular motions around the affected orbs. Then he gently laid his stick, or wand, on each eyebrow. As he did so, he quietly encouraged Maria Theresia to report any changes or movements she experienced within her. Then he placed a magnet on each temple. Immediately, he felt a sudden sensation of heat upon her cheeks, which the girl confirmed; he also observed a redness in the skin and a trembling of the limbs. She then described a gathering force at the base of her neck which was compelling her head backwards and upwards. As these movements occurred, M—— noted that the spasms in her eyes were more marked and at times convulsive. Then, as this brief crisis came to its end, the redness left her cheeks, her head resumed its normal position, the trembling ceased, and it appeared to M—— that her eyes were in a better alignment, and also less swollen.

He repeated the procedure each day at the same time, and each day the brief crisis led to an evident improvement, until by the end of the fourth day the proper alignment of her eyes had returned and no extrusion was to be remarked. The left eye appeared to be smaller than the right, but as the treatment continued, their sizes began to balance. The girl's parents were amazed: M——'s promise had been fulfilled, and their daughter no longer showed the deformity which might alarm those who watched her play. M——, however, was already preoccupied with the patient's internal condition, which he judged to be moving towards the necessary crisis. As he continued his daily procedures, she reported the presence of sharp pains in the occiput which penetrated the whole of her head. The pain then followed the optic nerve, producing constant pinpricks as it travelled and multiplied across the retina. These symptoms were accompanied by nervous jerkings of the head.

For many years, Maria Theresia had lost all sense of smell, and her nose produced no mucus. Now, suddenly, there was a visible swelling of the nasal passages, and a forceful discharge of green, viscous matter. Shortly afterwards, to the patient's further embarrassment, there were additional discharges, this time in the form of copious diarrhoea. The pains in her eyes continued, and she reported feelings of vertigo. M—— recognised that she was at a time of maximum vulnerability. A crisis was never a neutral occurrence: it might be benign or malign—not in its nature, but in its consequences, leading either to progress or regress. He therefore proposed to the girl's parents that she take up residence for a short period at 261 Landstrasse. She would be looked after by M——'s wife, though she could bring her own maid if necessary. There were already two young female patients established in the household, so questions of decorum need not arise. This new plan was swiftly agreed.

On Maria Theresia's second day in the house, and still in the presence of her father, M——, after touching her face and skull as before, placed the patient in front of a mirror. Taking his wand, he pointed it at her reflection. Then, as he moved the wand, the girl's head slightly turned, as if following its movements in the glass. M——, sensing that Herr von P—— was about to give tongue to his astonishment, quieted him with a gesture.

"You are aware that you are moving your head?"

"I am."

"Is there a reason why you are moving your head?"

"It is as if I am following something."

"Is it a noise that you are following?"

"No, not a noise."

"Is it a smell that you are following?"

"I still have no sense of smell. I am merely . . . following. That is all I can say."

"It is enough."

M—— assured Herr von P—— that his house would always be open to him and his wife, but that he expected progress in the ensuing days to be slow. In truth, he judged the girl's cure more likely if he could treat her without the presence of a father who struck him as overbearing, and a mother who, perhaps by reason of her Italian blood, seemed liable to hysteria. It was still just possible that Maria Theresia's blindness was caused by atrophy of the optic nerve, in which case there was nothing that magnetism, or any other known procedure, could do for her. But M—— doubted this. The convulsions he had witnessed, and the symptoms reported, all spoke of a disturbance to the whole nervous system due to some powerful shock. In the absence of any witnesses at the time, or of the patient's memory, it was impossible to determine what kind of shock it might have been. This did not perturb M—— unduly: it was the effect he was treating, not the cause. Indeed, it might be fortunate that the Fräulein could not recall the precise nature of the precipitating event.

In the preceding two years, it had become increasingly apparent to M—— that in bringing the patient to the necessary point of crisis, the touch of the human hand was of central, animating importance. At first, his touching of the patient at the moment of magnetism was designed to be calming, or at best emphatic. If, for instance, magnets were placed on either side of the ear, it seemed a natural gesture to stroke that ear in a manner confirming the realignment being sought. But M—— could not help observing that when all favourable conditions for cure had been created, with a circle of patients around the baquet in the soft candlelight, it was often the case that when he, as a musician, removed his fingers from the rotating glass armonica and then, as a physician, laid them on the afflicted part of the body, the patient might be instantly brought to crisis. M—— was at times inclined to ponder how much was the effect of the magnetism, and how much that of the magnetiser himself. Maria Theresia was not apprised of such wider considerations, any more than she was asked to join other patients around the oaken tub.

"Your treatment causes pain."

"No. What is causing pain is that you are beginning to see. When you look in the mirror you see the wand I am holding and turn your head to follow it. You say yourself that there is a shape moving."

"But you are treating me. And I am feeling pain."

"The pain is a sign of a beneficial response to the crisis. The pain shows that your optic nerve and retina, so long abandoned from use, are becoming active again."

"Other doctors have told me that the pain they were inflicting was necessary and beneficial. You are a doctor of philosophy as well?"

"I am."

"Philosophers can explain anything away."

M—— took no offence, indeed was pleased with such an attitude.

Such was the girl's new susceptibility to light that he had to bind her eyes with a triple bandage, which remained in place at all times when she was not being treated. He had begun by presenting to her, at a certain distance, objects of the same kind which were either white or black. She was able to perceive the black objects without distress, but flinched at the white objects, reporting that the pain they produced in her eyes was like that of a soft brush being drawn across the retina; they also provoked a sense of giddiness. M—— therefore removed all the white objects.

Next, he introduced her to the intermediate colours. Maria Theresia was able to distinguish between them, though unable to describe how they appeared to her—except for the colour black, which was, she said, the picture of her former blindness. When the colours were ascribed their names, she often failed to apply the correct name the next time a colour was shown. Nor was she able to calculate the distance objects were from her, imagining them all to be within reach; thus she extended her hands to pick up items twenty feet away. It was also the case, in these early days, that the impression an object left upon her retina lasted for up to a minute. She was obliged, therefore, to cover her eyes with her hands until the impression faded, else it would become confused with the next object presented to her view. Further, since the muscles of the eye had fallen into disuse, she had no practice at moving her gaze, searching for objects, focusing upon them and accounting for their position.

Neither was it the case that the elation felt by both M—— and the girl's parents when she first began to perceive light and forms was shared by the patient herself. What had come into her life was not, as she had expected, a panorama of the world so long concealed from her, and so long described by others; still less was there an understanding of that world. Instead, a greater confusion was now heaped upon the confusion that already existed— a state exacerbated by the ocular pains and feelings of vertigo. The melancholia that was the obverse of her natural cheerfulness came much to the fore at this time.

Understanding this, M—— resolved to slow the pace of his treatment; also, to make the hours of leisure and rest as pleasant as possible. He encouraged intimacy with the other two young women living in the household: Fräulein Ossine, the eighteen-year-old daughter of an army officer, who suffered from purulent phthisis and irritable melancholia; and the nineteen-year-old Zwelferine, struck blind at the age of two, whom M—— had found in an orphanage and was treating at his own expense. Each had something in common with one of the others: Maria Theresia and Fräulein Ossine were both of good family and imperial pension holders; Maria Theresia and Zwelferine were both blind; Zwelferine and Fräulein Ossine were both given to the periodic vomiting of blood.

Such company was a useful distraction; but M—— believed that Maria Theresia also needed several hours in the day devoted to a peaceful and familiar routine. He therefore took to sitting with her, talking of subjects far from her immediate concern, and reading to her from his library. Sometimes they would play music together, she with bandaged eyes at the klavier, he on the violoncello.

He also used this time to know the girl better, to assess her truthfulness, her memory, and her temperament. He noted that even when her spirits ran high, she was never headstrong; she showed neither the arrogance of her father nor the wilfulness of her mother.

He might ask, "What would you like to do this afternoon?"

And she would reply, "What do you propose?"

Or he might ask, "What would you like to play?"

And she would reply, "What would you like me to play?"

When such courtesies were finished with, he discovered that she had clear opinions, arrived at through the use of reason. But he also concluded that, even beyond the normal obedience of children, Maria Theresia was accustomed to doing as she was instructed: by her parents, her teachers, her doctors. She played beautifully, with a fine memory, and it seemed to M—— that it was only when she was at the klavier, immersed in a piece familiar to her, that she truly felt free, and allowed herself to be playful, expressive, thoughtful. It struck him, as he watched her profile, her bandaged eyes, and her firm, upright posture, that his enterprise was not without some danger. Was it possible that her talent, and the pleasure she evidently took in it, might be tied to her blindness in a way he could not fully understand? And then, as he followed her hands moving in their practised, easy man-ner, sometimes strong and springy, at others as leisurely as ferns wafted by a breeze, he found himself wondering how the first sight of a keyboard might affect her. Might the white keys throw her into turmoil, the black ones remind her only of blindness?

Their daily work continued. So far, Maria Theresia had been

presented with a mere sequence of static objects: his concern had been to establish and accustom her to shape, colour, location, distance. Now he decided to introduce the concept of movement, and with it the reality of a human face. Though she was well used to M——'s voice, he had so far always kept out of her lines of perception. Gently, he undid the bandages, asking her immediately to cover her eyes with her hands. Then he came round to face her, placing himself at a distance of a few feet. Telling her to take away her hands, he began slowly turning his head from one profile through to its opposite.

She laughed. And then placed the hands she had removed from her eyes over her mouth. M——'s excitement as a physician overcame his vanity as a man that he should provoke such a reaction in her. Then she took her hands from her mouth, placed them over her eyes, and after a few seconds released them and looked at him again. And laughed again.

"What is that?" she asked, pointing.

"This?"

"Yes, that." She was giggling to herself in a manner which, in other circumstances, he would have judged uncivil.

"It is a nose."

"It is ridiculous."

"You are the only person cruel enough to have made that observation," he said, pretending to be piqued. "Others have found it acceptable, even agreeable."

"Are all . . . noses like that?"

"There are differences, but, charming Fräulein, I must warn you that this is by no means anything out of the ordinary, as far as noses go."

"Then I shall have much cause for laughter. I must tell Zwelferine about noses."

He decided on an additional experiment. Maria Theresia had always enjoyed the presence, and the affection, of the house dog, a large, amiable beast of uncertain species. Now M—— went to the curtained door, opened it slightly, and whistled.

Twenty seconds later, Maria Theresia was saying, "Oh, a dog is a much more pleasing sight than a man."

"You are, sadly, not alone in that opinion."

There followed a period when her improving sight led to greater cheerfulness, while her clumsiness and error in the face of this newly discovered world drew her down into melancholy. One evening M—— took her outside into the darkened garden and suggested that she tip her head backwards. That night the heavens were blazing. M—— briefly found himself thinking: black and white again, though happily much more black than white. But Maria Theresia's reaction took any anxiety away. She stood there in astonishment, head back, mouth open, turning from time to time, pointing, not saying a word. She ignored his offer to identify the constellations; she did not want words to interfere with her sense of wonder, and continued looking until her neck hurt. From that evening on, visual phenomena of any distinction were automatically compared to a starry sky—and found wanting.

Though each morning M—— continued his treatment in exactly the same way, he now did so with a kind of feigned concentration. Within himself he was debating between two lines of thought, and between two parts of his intellectual formation. The doctor of philosophy argued that the universal element which underlay everything had surely now been laid bare in the form of magnetism. The doctor of medicine argued that magnetism had less to do with the patient's progress than the power of touch, and that even the laying on of hands was merely emblematic, as was the application of magnets and of the wand. What was actually happening was some collaboration or complicity between physician and patient, so that his presence and authority were permitting the patient to cure herself. He did not mention this second explanation to anyone, least of all the patient.

Maria Theresia's parents were as astonished by the further improvement in their daughter as she was by the starry heavens. As the news spread, friends and well-wishers began to turn up at 261 Landstrasse to witness the miracle. Passersby often lingered outside the house, hoping to glimpse the famous patient; while letters requesting her physician's attendance at sickbeds across the city arrived each day. At first M—— was happy to allow Maria Theresia to demonstrate her ability to distinguish colours and shapes, even if some of her naming was not yet faultless. But such performances palpably tired her, and he severely restricted the number of visitors. This sudden ruling had the effect of increasing both the rumours of miracle working and the suspicions harboured by some fellow members of the Faculty of Medicine. The case was also beginning to make the Church uneasy, since the popular understanding was that M—— had only to touch the afflicted part of a sick person for the sickness to be healed. That anyone other than Jesus Christ might effect a cure by the laying on of hands struck many of the clergy as blasphemous.

M—— was aware of these rumours, but felt confident in the backing of Professor Stoerk, who had come to 261 Landstrasse and been officially impressed by the working of the new cure. What then did it matter if other members of the Faculty muttered against him, or even dropped the slander that his patient's newfound ability to name colours and objects was in fact due to close training? The conservative, the slow-witted and the envious existed in every profession. In the longer term, once M——'s methods were understood and the number of cures increased, all men of reason would be obliged to believe him.

One day when Maria Theresia's state of mind was at its calmest, M—— invited her parents to attend him that afternoon. He then proposed to his patient that she take up her instrument, unaccompanied and unbandaged. She enthusiastically agreed, and the four of them proceeded to the music room. Chairs were set out for Herr von P—— and his wife, while M—— took a stool close to the klavier, the better to observe Maria Theresia's hands, eyes and moral condition. She took several deep breaths and then, after a barely endurable pause, the first notes of a sonata by Haydn fell upon their ears.

It was a disaster. You might have thought the girl a novice and the sonata a piece she had never played. The fingering was inept, the rhythms flawed; all grace and wit and tenderness vanished from the music. When the first movement stumbled to a confused halt, there was a silence during which M—— could sense the parents exchanging glances. Then, suddenly, the same music began again, now confidently, brightly, perfectly. He looked across at the parents, but they in turn had eyes only for their daughter. Turning towards the klavier, M—— realised the cause of this sudden excellence: the girl had her eyes tightly closed and her chin raised high above the keyboard.

When Maria Theresia reached the end of the movement, she opened her eyes, looked down, and went back to the beginning. The result, again, was chaos, and this time M—— thought he guessed the reason: she was following her hands transfixedly. And it seemed that the very act of watching was destroying her skill. Fascinated by her own fingers, and the way they moved across the keyboard, she was unable to bring them under her full control. She observed their disobedience until the end of the movement, then rose and ran to the door.

There was yet another silence.

Eventually, M—— said, "It is to be expected."

Herr von P——, red with anger, replied, "It is a catastrophe."

"It will take time. Every day there will be an improvement."

"It is a catastrophe. If news of this gets out, it will be the end of her career."

Unwisely, M—— put the question, "Would you rather your daughter could see, or could play?"

Herr von P——, now choleric, was on his feet, with his wife beside him. "It was not, sir, a choice I remember you offering when we brought her to you."

After they left, M—— found the girl in a deplorable condition. He sought to reassure her, telling her it was no surprise that the sight of her fingers disconcerted her playing.

"If it was no surprise, why did you not warn me?"

He reminded her that her sight had been improving on an almost daily basis, and so it was inevitable that her playing would also improve, once she became accustomed to the presence of her fingers on the keys.

"That is why I played the piece a third time. And it was even worse than the first."

M—— did not argue the point. He knew from his own experience how, in matters of art, the nerves occupied a vital part. If you played badly, your spirits fell; if your spirits were low, you played worse—and so, decliningly, on. Instead, M—— pointed to the wider improvement in Maria Theresia's condition. This did not satisfy her either.

"In my darkness, music was my entire consolation. To be brought into the light and then lose the ability to play would be cruel justice."

"That will not happen. It is not a choice. You must trust me that such will not be the case."

He looked at her, and followed the development, and the departure, of a frown. Eventually, she replied, "Apart from the matter of pain, you have always been worthy of trust. What you have said might happen has happened. Therefore, yes, I trust you."

In the following days, M—— was made aware that his earlier dismissal of the outside world's opinion had been naive. A proposal arrived from certain members of the Faculty of Medicine that endorsement of the practice of magnetic healing should only be given if M—— could reproduce his effects with a new patient, under full lighting and in the presence of six Faculty examiners—conditions which would, M—— knew, destroy its effectiveness. Satirical tongues were already asking if in the future all doctors would be equipped with magic wands. More dangerously, some were questioning the moral wisdom of the procedure. Did it help the status and respectability of the profession if one of their number took young women into his household, cloistered them behind drawn curtains, and then laid hands upon them amid jars of magnetised water and to the caterwauling of a glass armonica?

On 29 April 177–, Frau von P—— was shown into M——'s study. She was clearly agitated, and refused to sit down.

"I have come to remove my daughter from you."

"Has she indicated that she wishes to cease her treatment?"

"*Her* wishes . . . That remark, sir, is an impertinence. *Her* wishes are subordinate to her parents' wishes."

M—— looked at her calmly. "Then I shall fetch her."

"No. Ring for a servant. I do not care for you to instruct her how to answer."

"Very well." He rang; Maria Theresia was fetched; she looked anxiously from one to the other.

"Your mother wishes you to cease treatment and return home."

"What is your opinion?"

"My opinion is that if this is what you wish, then I cannot oppose it."

"That was not what I asked. I was asking your medical opinion."

M—— glanced across at the mother. "My . . . medical opinion is that you are still at a precarious stage. I think it very possible that a complete cure may be effected. Equally, it is very possible that any gains made, once lost, could never be recovered."

"That is very clear. Then I choose to stay. I wish to stay."

The mother instantly began a display of stamping and shouting, the like of which M—— had never before encountered in the imperial city of V——. It was an outburst far beyond the natural expression of Frau von P——'s Italian blood, and might even have been comical, had not her nervous frenzy set off an answering spasm of convulsion in the daughter.

"Madam, I must ask you to control yourself," he said quietly.

But this enraged the mother even more, and with two sources of provocation in front of her, she continued to denounce her daughter's insolence, stubbornness and ingratitude. When M—— tried to lay a hand on her forearm, Frau von P—— turned on Maria Theresia, seized her, and threw her headlong into the wall. Above the women's screams, M—— summoned his staff, who held back the termagant just as she was about to set upon the doctor himself. Suddenly, another voice was added to the bedlam.

"Return my daughter! Resist me and you die!"

The door was thrown violently open, and Herr von P—— himself appeared, a framed figure with sword aloft. Hurling himself into the study, he threatened to cut to pieces anyone who opposed him.

"Then, sir, you will have to cut me to pieces," M—— answered firmly. Herr von P—— stopped, uncertain whether to attack the doctor, rescue his daughter, or console his wife. Unable to decide, he settled for repeating his threats. The daughter was weeping, the mother screaming, the physician attempting to argue rationally, the father noisily promising mayhem and death.

M—— remained dispassionate enough to reflect that the young Mozart would have happily set this operatic quartet to music.

Eventually, the father was pacified and then disarmed. He departed with malediction on his tongue, and seeming to forget his wife, who stood for a few moments looking from M——to her daughter and back again, before herself leaving. Immediately, and for the rest of the day, M—— sought to calm Maria Theresia. As he did so, he came to conclude that his initial presumption had been confirmed: Maria Theresia's blindness had certainly been a hysterical reaction to the equally hysterical behaviour of one or both of her parents. That a sensitive, artistic child, in the face of such an emotional assault, might instinctively close herself off from the world seemed reasonable, even inevitable. And the frenzied parents, having been responsible for the girl's condition in the first place, were now aggravating it.

What could have caused this sudden, destructive outburst? More, surely, than a mere flouting of parental will. M—— therefore tried to imagine it from their point of view. A child goes blind, all known cures fail until, after more than a dozen years, a new physician with a novel procedure begins to make her see again. The prognosis is optimistic, and the parents are rewarded at last for their love, wisdom, and medical courage. But then the girl plays, and their world is turned upside down. Before, they had been in charge of a blind virtuoso; now, sight had rendered her mediocre. If she continued playing like that, her career would be over. But even assuming that she rediscovered all her former skill, she would lack the originality of being blind. She would be merely one pianist among many others. And there would be no reason for the empress to continue her pension. Two hundred gold ducats had made a difference to their lives, and how, without it, would they commission works from leading composers?

M—— understood such a dilemma, but it could not be his primary concern. He was a physician, not a musical impresario.

In any case, he was convinced that once Maria Theresia became accustomed to the sight of her hands on a keyboard, once observation ceased altering her performance, her skill would not merely return, but develop and improve. For how could it possibly be an advantage to be blind? Furthermore, the girl had chosen openly to defy her parents and continue the cure. How could he disappoint her hopes? Even if it meant distributing cudgels to his servants, he would defend her right to live under his roof.

Yet it was not just the frenzied parents who were threatening the household. Opinion at court and in society had turned against the physician who had walled up a young woman and now refused to return her to her parents. That the girl herself also refused did not help M——'s case: in the eyes of some it merely confirmed him as a magician, a bewitcher whose hypnotic powers might not cure, but could certainly enslave. Moral fault and medical fault intertwined, giving birth to scandal. Such a miasma of innuendo arose in the imperial city that Professor Stoerk was provoked into action. Withdrawing his previous endorsement of M——'s activities, he now wrote, on 2 May 177–, demanding that M—— cease his "imposture" and return the girl.

Again, M—— refused. Maria Theresia von P——, he replied, was suffering from convulsions and delirious imaginings. A court physician was sent to examine her, and reported to Stoerk that in his opinion the patient was in no condition to be sent back. Thus reprieved, M—— spent the next weeks devoting himself entirely to her case. With words, with magnetism, with the touch of his hands, and with her belief in him, he succeeded in bringing her nervous hysteria under control within nine days. Better still, it presently became evident that her perception was now sharper than at any previous time, suggesting that the pathways of the eye and brain had become strengthened. He did not yet ask her if she wanted to play; nor did she suggest it.

M—— knew that it would not be possible to keep Maria

Theresia von P—— until she was fully cured, but did not wish to surrender her until she had acquired sufficient robustness to hold the world at bay. After five weeks of siege, an agreement was reached: M—— would return the girl to her parents' care, and they would allow M—— to continue treating her as and when it might be necessary. With this peace treaty in place, Maria Theresia was handed over on 8 June 177–.

That was the last day on which M—— saw her. At once, the von P——s reneged on their word, keeping their daughter in close custody, and forbidding all contact with M——. We cannot know what was said, or done, in that household, we can know only its predictable consequence: Maria Theresia von P—— relapsed immediately into blindness, a condition from which she was not to emerge in the remaining forty-seven years of her life.

We have no account of Maria Theresia's anguish, of her moral suffering and mental reflection. But the world of constant darkness was at least familiar to her. We may presume that she gave up all hope of cure, and also of escape from her parents; we may know that she took up her career again, first as pianist and singer, then as composer, and eventually as teacher. She learnt the use of a composition board invented for her by her amanuensis and librettist, Johann Riedinger; she also owned a hand-printing machine for her correspondence. Her fame spread across Europe; she knew sixty concertos by heart, and played them in Prague, London and Berlin.

As for M——, he was driven from the imperial city of V—— by the Faculty of Medicine and the Committee to Sustain Morality, a combination which ensured that he was remembered there as half charlatan, half seducer. He withdrew first to Switzerland, and then established himself in Paris. In 178–, seven years after they had last seen one another, Maria Theresia von P—— came to perform in the French capital. At the Tuileries, before Louis XVI and Marie Antoinette, she introduced the concerto Mozart had written for her. She and M—— did not meet; nor can we tell if either of them would have desired such a meeting. Maria Theresia lived on in darkness, usefully, celebratedly, until her death in 182–.

M—— had died nine years previously, at the age of eighty-one, his intellectual powers and musical enthusiasm both undiminished. As he lay dying at Meersburg, on the shores of Lake Constance, he sent for his young friend F——, a seminarist, to play for him on the glass armonica which had accompanied him through all his travels since he left 261 Landstrasse. According to one account, the pangs of his dying were soothed by listening a final time to the music of the spheres. According to another, the young seminarist was delayed, and M—— died before F—— could touch his chalky fingers to the rotating glass.

# Carcassonne

IN THE SUMMER of 1839, a man puts a telescope to his eye and inspects the Brazilian coastal town of Laguna. He is a foreign guerrilla leader whose recent success has brought the surrender of the imperial fleet. The liberator is on board its captured flagship, a seven-gun topsail schooner called the *Itaparica*, now at anchor in the lagoon from which the town gets its name. The telescope offers a view of a hilly quarter known as the Barra, containing a few simple but picturesque buildings. Outside one of them sits a woman. At the sight of her, the man, as he later put it, "forthwith gave orders for the boat to be got out, as I wished to go ashore."

Anita Riberas was eighteen, of mixed Portuguese and Indian descent, with dark hair, large breasts, "a virile carriage and determined face." She would have known the guerrilla's name, since he had helped free her native town. But his search for both the young woman and her house was in vain, until he chanced upon a shopkeeper of his acquaintance who invited him in for coffee. And there, as if waiting for him, she was. "We both remained enraptured and silent, gazing on one another like two people who meet not for the first time, and seek in each other's faces something which makes it easier to recall the forgotten past." That's how he put it, many years later, in his autobiography, where he mentions an additional reason for their enraptured silence: he had very little Portuguese, and she no Italian. So he spoke his eventual greeting in his own language: "*Tu devi esser mia.*" You must be mine. His words transcended the problem of immediate understanding: "I had formed a tie, pronounced a decree, which death alone can annul."

Is there a more romantic encounter than this? And since Garibaldi was one of the last romantic heroes of European history, let's not quibble over circumstantial detail. For instance, he must have been able to speak passable Portuguese, since he'd been fighting in Brazil for years; for instance, Anita, despite her age, was no shy maiden but a woman already married for several years to a local cobbler. Let's also forget about a husband's heart and a family's honour, about whether violence occurred or money was exchanged when, a few nights later, Garibaldi came ashore and carried Anita off. Instead, let's just agree that it was what both parties deeply and instantly desired, and that in places and times where justice is approximate, possession is usually nine points of the law.

They were married in Montevideo three years later, having heard reports that the cobbler might be dead. According to the historian G. M. Trevelyan, they "spent their honeymoon in amphibious warfare along the coast and in the lagoon, fighting at close quarters against desperate odds." As good on a horse as he, and as brave, she was his companion in war and marriage for ten years; to his troops she was mascot, invigorator, nurse. The birth of four children did not impede her devotion to the republican cause, first in Brazil, then Uruguay, and, finally, Europe. She was with Garibaldi in the defence of the Roman Republic, and, after its defeat, in his retreat across the Papal States to the Adriatic coast. During their flight she fell mortally ill. Garibaldi, though urged to flee by himself, stayed with his wife; together they dodged the Austrian white-coats in the marshes around Ravenna. In her final days, Anita held resolutely to "the undogmatic religion of her husband," a fact which draws from Trevelyan a tremendous romantic flourish: "Dying on the breast of Garibaldi, she needed no priest."

Some years ago, at a booksellers' conference in Glasgow, I found myself talking to two Australian women, a novelist and a cook. Or rather, listening, since they were discussing the effect of different foods on the taste of a man's sperm. "Cinnamon," said the novelist knowingly. "No, not just by itself," replied the cook. "You need strawberries, blackberries and cinnamon, that's the best." She added that she could always tell a meat eater. "Believe me, I know. I did a blind tasting once." Hesitant about contributing to the conversation, I mentioned asparagus. "Yes," replied the cook. "It shows in the urine but it also shows in the ejaculate." If I hadn't written the exchange down shortly afterwards, I might think I was remembering part of some hot dream.

A psychiatrist friend of mine maintains that there is a direct correlation between interest in food and interest in sex. The lustful gourmand is almost a cliché; while aversion to food is often accompanied by erotic indifference. As for the normal, middle part of the spectrum: I can think of people who, because of the circles in which they move, exaggerate their interest in food; often, they are the same sort of people who (again, because of peer pressure) might claim more of an interest in sex than they actually feel. Counterexamples come to mind: couples whose appetite for food, and cooking, and eating out, has come to supplant the appetite for sex, and for whom bed, after a meal, is a place of repose, not activity. But on the whole, I'd say there's something to this theory.

The expectation of an experience governs and distorts the experience itself. I may not know anything about sperm tasting, but I know about wine tasting. If someone puts a glass of wine in front of you, it is impossible to approach it without preconceptions. To begin with, you might not actually like the stuff. But allowing that you do, then many subliminal factors come into play before you've even taken a sip. What colour the wine is, what it smells like, what glass it is in, how much it costs, who's paying for it, where you are, what your mood is, whether or not you've had this wine before. It is impossible to factor out such preknowledge. The only way to get round it is an extreme one. If you are blindfolded, and someone puts a clothes-peg on your nose, and hands you a glass of wine, then, even if you are the greatest expert in the world, you will be unable to tell the most basic things about it. Not even whether it is red or white.

Of all our senses, it is the one with the broadest application, from a brief impression on the tongue to a learned aesthetic response to a painting. It is also the one that most describes us. We may be better or worse people, happy or miserable, successful or failing, but what we *are*, within these wider categories, how we define ourselves, as opposed to how we are genetically defined, is what we call "taste." Yet the word—perhaps because of its broad catchment area—easily misleads. "Taste" can imply calm reflection; while its derivatives—tasteful, tastefulness, tasteless, tastelessness—lead us into a world of minute differentiations, of snobbery, social values and soft furnishings. True taste, essential taste, is much more instinctual and unreflecting. It says, Me, here, now, this, you. It says, Lower the boat and row me ashore. Dowell, the narrator of Ford Madox Ford's *The Good Soldier*, says of Nancy Rufford: "I just wanted to marry her as some people want to go to Carcassonne." Falling in love is the most violent expression of taste known to us.

And yet our language doesn't seem to represent that moment very well. We have no equivalent for "*coup de foudre,*" the lightning strike and thunderclap of love. We talk about there being "electricity" between a couple—but this is a domestic, not cosmic image, as if the pair should be practical and wear rubber soles to their shoes. We talk of "love at first sight," and indeed it happens, even in England, but the phrase makes it sound rather a polite business. We say that their eyes met across a crowded room. Again, how social it sounds. Across a crowded room. Across a crowded harbour.

Anita Riberas didn't, in fact, die "on the breast of Garibaldi," but rather more mundanely, and less like a lithograph. She died while the liberator and three of his followers, each holding a corner of her mattress, were moving her from a cart into a farmhouse. Still, we should celebrate that moment with the telescope and all it led to. Because this is the moment—the moment of passionate taste—that we are after. Few of us have telescopes and harbours available, and in the rewinding of memory we may discover that even the deepest and longest love relationships rarely start with full recognition, with "you must be mine" pronounced in a foreign tongue. The moment itself may be disguised as something else: admiration, pity, office camaraderie, shared danger, a common sense of justice. Perhaps it is too alarming a moment to be looked in the face at the time; so perhaps the English language is right to avoid Gallic flamboyance. I once asked a man who had been long and happily married where he had met his wife. "At an office party," he replied. And what had been his first impression of her? "I thought she was very nice," he replied.

So how do we know to trust that moment of passionate taste, however camouflaged? We don't, even if we feel we must, that this is all we have to go on. A woman friend once told me, "If you took me into a crowded room and there was one man with 'Nutter' tattooed on his forehead, I'd walk straight across to him." Another, twice-married friend confided, "I've thought of leaving my marriage, but I'm so bad at choosing that I wouldn't have any confidence I'd do better next time, and that would be a depressing thing to learn." Who or what can help us in the moment that sets the wild echoes flying? What do we trust: the sight of a woman's feet in walking boots, the novelty of a foreign accent, a loss of blood to the fingertips followed by exasperated self-criticism? I once went to visit a young married couple whose new house was astonishingly empty of furniture. "The problem," the wife explained, "is that he's got no taste at all and I've only got bad taste." I suppose that to accuse yourself of bad taste implies the latent presence of some sort of good taste. But in our love choices, few of us know whether or not we are going to end up in that house without furniture.

When I first became part of a couple, I began to examine with more self-interest the progress and fate of other couples. By now I was in my early thirties, and some of my contemporaries who had met a decade earlier were already beginning to break up. I realised that the two couples whose relationships seemed to resist time, whose partners continued to show joyful interest in one another, were both—all four—gay men in their sixties. This may have been just a statistical oddity; but I used to wonder if there was a reason. Was it because they had avoided the long travail of parenthood, which often grinds down heterosexual relationships? Possibly. Was it something essential to their gayness? Probably not, judging from gay couples of my own generation. One thing separating these two couples from the rest was that for many years and in many countries their relationship would have been illegal. A bond made in such circumstances may well run deeper: I am committing my safety into your hands, every day of our lives together. Perhaps there is a literary comparison: books written under oppressive regimes are often more highly valued than books written in societies where everything is permitted. Not that a writer should therefore pray for oppression, or a lover for illegality.

"I just wanted to marry her as some people want to go to Carcassonne." The first couple, T and H, met during the 1930s. T was from the English upper-middle classes, handsome, talented and modest. H came from a Jewish family in Vienna, who were so hard up that when he was a small boy (and his father at the First World War), his mother gave him away to the poorhouse for several years. Later, as a young man, he met the daughter of an English textile magnate, who helped get him out of Austria before the Second World War. In England, H worked for the family firm, and became engaged to the daughter. Then H met T under circumstances which T, rather coyly, refused to specify, but which were life-changing from the start. "Of course," T told me after H's death, "all this was very new to me—I hadn't been to bed with anybody at all."

What, you might ask, about H's deserted fiancée? But this is a happy story: T told me that she had "a very good instinct" for what was going on; that in due course she fell in love with someone else; and that the four of them became close and lifelong friends. H went on to become a successful clothes designer for a high-street chain, and on his death—given the liberal nature of this employer—T, who for decades had committed many illegal acts with his "Austrian friend," found himself in receipt of a widow's pension. When he told me all this, not long before his own death, two things struck me. The first was how dispassionately he narrated his own story; all his strongest emotions were aroused by the misfortunes and injustices of H's life before the two of them had met. And the second was a phrase he used when describing the arrival of H into his life. T said he was very bewildered, "But sure of one thing: I was determined to marry H."

The other couple, D and D, were South African. D1 was formal, shy, highly cultured; D2 more flamboyant, more obviously gay, full of teasing and double entendres. They lived in Cape Town, had a house on Santorini, and travelled widely. They had worked out how to live together down to the smallest detail: I remember them in Paris, explaining that as soon as they got to Europe they would always buy a large pannetone, on which to breakfast in their hotel room. (A couple's first task, it has always seemed to me, is to solve the problem of breakfast; if this can be worked out amicably, most other difficulties can too.) On one occasion D2 came to London by himself. Late in the evening, after drink had been taken, and we were talking about provincial France, he suddenly confessed, "I had the best fucky-fuck of my life in Carcassonne." It was not a line you would easily forget, particularly since he described how there had been a storm brewing, and at what the French call *le moment suprême*, there was an enormous roll of thunder overhead—a *coup de foudre* indeed. He didn't say he had been with D1 at the time, and because he didn't, I assumed he hadn't. After he died, I put his words into a novel, though with some hesitation about the accompanying weather, which raised the frequent literary problem of the *vrai* versus the *vraisemblable*. Life's astonishments are frequently literature's clichés. A couple of years later, I was on the phone to D1 when he alluded to this line and asked where I had got it from. Worrying at my possible betrayal, I admitted that D2 had been my source. "Ach," said D1 with sudden warmth, "we had such a *wonderful* time in Carcassonne." I felt relief; also a kind of surrogate nostalgia about the fact that they had been together.

For some, the sunlight catches on the telescope out there in the lagoon; for others, not. We choose, we are chosen, we are unchosen. I said to my friend who always picked nutters that maybe she should look for a nice nutter. She replied, "But how could I tell one?" Like most people, she believed what lovers told her until there was a good reason not to. For several years she went out with a nutter who always left promptly for the office; only towards the end of the relationship did she discover that his first appointment of the day was always with his shrink. I said, "You've just had bad luck." She said, "I don't want it to be luck. If it's luck, there's nothing I can do about it." People say that in the end you get what you deserve, but that phrase cuts both ways. People say that in modern cities there are too many terrific women and too many terrible men. The city of Carcassonne looks solid and enduring, but what we admire is mostly nineteenth-century reconstruction. Forget the hazard of "whether it will last," and whether longevity is in any case a virtue, a reward, an accommodation or another piece of luck. How much do we act, and how much are we acted upon, in that moment of passionate taste?

And we shouldn't forget that Garibaldi had a second wife (also a third—though we may ignore her). His ten years of marriage to Anita Riberas were followed by ten years of widowhood. Then, in the summer of 1859, during his Alpine campaign, he was fighting near Varese when a message was brought to him through the Austrian lines by a seventeen-year-old girl driving alone in a gig. She was Giuseppina Raimondi, the illegitimate daughter of Count Raimondi. Garibaldi was immediately smitten, wrote her a passionate letter, declared his love on bended knee. He admitted the difficulties to any union between them: he was nearly three times her age, already had another child by a peasant woman, and feared that Giuseppina's aristocratic background might not play well with his political image. But he convinced himself (and her), to the extent that on 3 December 1859, as a later historian than Trevelyan worded it, "She put aside her doubts and entered his room. The deed was done!" Like Anita, she was evidently dashing and brave; on 24 January 1860, they were married—in this instance, with the full dogma of the Catholic Church.

Tennyson met Garibaldi on the Isle of Wight four years later. The poet greatly admired the liberator, but also noted that he had "the divine stupidity of a hero." This second marriage—or rather, Garibaldi's illusions about it—lasted (according to which authority you believe) either a few hours or a few days, the time it took for the bridegroom to receive a letter detailing his new wife's past. Giuseppina, it turned out, had begun taking lovers at the age of eleven; she had married Garibaldi only at the insistence of her father; she had spent the night before her wedding with her most recent lover, by whom she was pregnant; and she had precipitated sexual events with her husband-to-be so that she could write to him on 1 January and claim to be carrying his child.

Garibaldi demanded not just an immediate separation but an annulment. The romantic hero's deeply unromantic reasoning was that since he had slept with Giuseppina only before the wedding and not after, the marriage had technically not been consummated. The law was unimpressed by such sophistry, and Garibaldi's appeal to higher influences, including the king, also failed. The liberator found himself shackled to Giuseppina for the next twenty years.

In the end, the law is only ever defeated by lawyers; in place of the romantic telescope, the legal microscope. The freeing argument, when it was eventually found, ran like this: since

Garibaldi's marriage had been solemnised in territory nominally under Austrian control, the law governing it might therefore be construed as the Austrian civil code, under which an annulment was (and perhaps always had been) possible. So the hero-lover was saved by the very nation against whose rule he had been fighting at the time. The distinguished lawyer who proposed this ingenious solution had, back in 1860, prepared the legislative unification of Italy; now, he achieved the marital disunification of the nation's unifier. Let us salute the name of Pasquale Stanislao Mancini.

# Pulse

MY PARENTS were walking down a farm track in Italy about three years ago. I often imagine myself watching them, always from behind. My mother, greying hair pulled back in a bunch, would be wearing a loose-cut patterned blouse over slacks and open-toed sandals; my father has a short-sleeved shirt, khaki trousers and polished brown shoes. His shirt is properly ironed, with twin buttoned pockets and turnups, if that's the word, on the sleeves. He owns half a dozen shirts like this; they proclaim him a man on holiday. Nor do they give the least hint of athleticism; at best, they might look appropriate on a bowling green.

The two of them could be holding hands; this was something they did unselfconsciously, whether I was behind them, watching, or not. They are walking down this track somewhere in Umbria because they are investigating a roughly chalked sign offering *vino novello*. And they are on foot because they have looked at the depth of the hard clay ruts and decided not to risk their hire car. I would have argued that this was the point of renting a car; but my parents were a cautious couple in many ways.

The track runs between vineyards. As it makes a bend to the left, a rusting, hangarlike barn comes into view. In front of it is a concrete structure like an oversize compost bin: about six feet high and nine across, with no roof or front to it. When they are about thirty yards away, my mother turns to my father and pulls a face. She may even say, "Yuck," or something similar. My father frowns and doesn't reply. This was the first time it happened; or rather, to be exact, the first time he noticed it.

We live in what used to be a market town some thirty miles northwest of London. Mum works in hospital administration; Dad has been a solicitor in a local practice all his adult life. He says the work will see him out, but that his type of solicitor—not just a technician who understands documents, but a general giver of advice—won't exist in the future. The doctor, the vicar, the lawyer, perhaps the schoolmaster—in the old days, these were figures everyone turned to for more than just their professional competency. Nowadays, my father says, people do their own conveyancing, write their own wills, agree on the terms of their divorce beforehand, and take their own advice. If they want a second opinion, they prefer an agony aunt to a solicitor, and the Internet to both. My father takes this all philosophically, even when people imagine they're capable of pleading their own cases. He just smiles, and repeats the old legal saying: the man who represents himself in court has a fool for a client.

Dad advised me against following him into the law, so I did a BEd and now teach in a sixth-form college about fifteen miles away. But I didn't see any reason to leave the town where I grew up. I go to the local gym, and on Fridays run with a group led by my friend Jake; that's how I met Janice. She was always going to stand out in a place like this, because she has that London edge to her. I think she hoped I'd want to move to the big city, and was disappointed when I didn't. No, I don't think that; I know it.

Mum . . . who can describe their mother? It's like when interviewers ask one of the royals what it's like to be royal, and they laugh and say they don't know what it's like not to be royal. I don't know what it would be like for my mum not to be my mum. Because if she wasn't, then I wouldn't, I couldn't, be me, could I?

Apparently I had a difficult birth. Perhaps that's why there's only me; though I've never asked. We don't do gynaecology in our family. Or religion, because we don't have any. We do politics a bit, but rarely argue, since we think the parties are as bad as one another. Dad may be a bit more right-wing than Mum, but essentially we believe in self-reliance, helping others, and not expecting the state to look after us from cradle to grave. We pay our taxes and our pension contributions and have life assurance; we use the National Health Service and give to charity when we can. We're ordinary, sensible middle-class people.

And without Mum we wouldn't be any of it. Dad had a bit of a drink problem when I was little, but Mum sorted him out and turned him into a purely social drinker. I was classified as "disruptive" at school, but Mum sorted me out with patience and love, while making it clear exactly which lines I couldn't cross. I expect she did the same with Dad. She organises us. She still has a bit of her Lancashire accent left, but we don't do that silly north–south stuff in our family, not even as a joke. I also think it's different when there's only one child, because there aren't two natural teams, kids and adults. There are just the three of you, and though I might have been more coddled, I also learnt from an earlier age to live in an adult world, because that's the only game in town. I may be wrong about this. If you asked Janice if she thought I was fully grown up, I can imagine the answer.


So my mother pulls a face and my father frowns. They walk on until the contents of the concrete bin become clearer: a curving slope of purply-red muck. My mother—and I am guessing here, though her vocabulary is familiar to me—now says something like,

"Pretty whiffy."

My father can see what my mother's referring to: a pile of marc. That's the name, apparently, for what's left after grapes have been crushed—the discarded skins and stalks and pips and so on. My parents know about this sort of thing; in their non-fanatical way they are keen on their food and drink. That's why they were on this farm track in the first place—looking for a few bottles of that year's wine to take home. I'm not indifferent to food and drink, just regard them more pragmatically. I know which foods are healthiest and also most energy-providing. And I know precisely how much alcohol relaxes me and gives me a good time, and how much is too much. Jake, who is both fitter and more hedonistic than me, once told me what they say about martinis: "One's perfect. Two's too many. And three's not enough." Except in my case: I once ordered a martini—and half was just about right.

So my father approaches this great heap of detritus, stops about ten feet away and consciously sniffs. Nothing. Five feet—still nothing. Only when he puts his nose almost into the marc does anything register. Even so, it's just a faint version of the pungent smell his eyes—and his wife—tell him exists. My father's response is more one of curiosity than alarm. For the rest of the holiday he monitors the ways in which his nose lets him down. Benzene fumes when filling up the car—nothing. A double espresso in a village bar—nothing. Flowers cascading over a crumbly wall—nothing. The half-inch of wine a hovering waiter has poured into his glass—nothing. Soap, shampoo—nothing. Deodorant—nothing. That was the oddest thing of all, Dad told me: to be putting on deodorant and not be able to smell something you were putting on to stop something else you also couldn't smell.

They agreed there wasn't much point in doing anything until they got home. Mum expected she'd have to badger Dad to call the health centre. The two of them shared a reluctance to bother the doctor unless it was serious. But each thought something that happened to the other was more serious than if it was happening to them. Hence the necessity to badger. Eventually, one might simply ring up and book an appointment in the other's name.

This time, my father did it for himself. I asked what had decided him. He paused. "Well, if you want to know, son, it was when I realised I couldn't smell your mum."

"You mean, her perfume?"

"No, not her perfume. Her skin. Her . . . self."

There was a fond, absent look in his eye as he said it. I didn't find this at all embarrassing. He was just a man at ease with what he felt about his wife. There are some parents who make a display of marital emotion in front of their children: look at us, see how young we still are, how dashing, aren't we just the picture? My parents weren't like this at all. And I envied them the more for it, that they didn't need to show off.


When you run in our group, there's the leader, Jake, who sets the pace and also makes sure no one falls too far behind. At the front are the heavy guys who keep their heads down, check their watches and heart monitors, and talk, if at all, about hydration levels and how many calories they've done. At the back are those who aren't fit enough to run and talk at the same time. And in between are the rest of us, who like both the exercise and the chat. But there's a rule: no one's allowed to monopolise anyone else, not even if they're going out together. So one Friday evening, I checked my stride to fall in with Janice, our newest recruit. Her running gear had clearly not been bought at the local shop where the rest of us go; it was looser cut, and silkier, and had needless bits of piping on it.

"So what brings you to our town?"

"Been here two years, actually."

"So what brought you to our town?"

She ran a few yards. "Boyfriend." Ah. Then a few more yards. "Ex-boyfriend." Ah, better—maybe she's running him off. But I didn't like to probe. Anyway, there's another rule in the group: keep it light when you're running. No British foreign policy, and no big emotional stuff either. Sometimes it makes us sound like a bunch of hairdressers, but it's a useful rule.

"Only a couple more k."

"So be it."

"Fancy a drink afterwards?"

She looked across and up at me. "So be it," she repeated with a grin.

She was easy to talk to, mainly because I did all the listening. And more of the looking too. She was slim, neat, black-haired, well manicured, with a slightly off-centre tweak to her nose that I found instantly sexy. She was in motion a lot, gesturing, flicking at her hair, looking away, looking back; I found this exhilarating. She told me she worked in London as PA to the section head of a women's magazine I'd just about heard of.

"Do you get lots of free samples?"

She stopped and looked at me; I didn't know her well enough to tell if she was really put out or just pretending. "I can't believe that's the first question you ask me about my job."

It had seemed reasonable enough to me. "OK," I replied, "let's pretend I've already asked you fourteen acceptable questions about your job. Question fifteen: do you get lots of free samples?"

She laughed. "Do you always do things in the wrong order?"

"Only if it makes someone laugh," I replied.


My parents were plump, and good advertisements for plumpness. They took little exercise, and their response to having a big lunch was to lie down and sleep it off. They treated my fitness

programme as a youthful eccentricity: the only time they reacted
as if I was fifteen rather than thirty. In their view, serious exercise
was appropriate only for people like soldiers, firemen and the
police. Once, up in London, they had found themselves outside
one of those gyms which let you glimpse some of the activities
within. It's meant to be alluring, but my parents were horrified.

"They all looked so *solemn*," my mother said.

"And most of them had earphones and were listening to
music. Or watching TV screens. As if the only way to concentrate
on getting fit was not to concentrate on it."

"They were ruled by those machines, ruled."

I knew better than to try and convince my parents of the plea-
sures and rewards of exercise, from increased mental alertness to
heightened sexual capacity. I'm not boasting, I promise. It's true,
it's well documented. Jake, who goes on hiking holidays with a
succession of girlfriends, told me about a paradox he'd discovered. He said that if you walk for, say, three or four hours, you
build up a good appetite, enjoy a nice dinner, and as often as not
fall asleep as soon as you get into bed. Whereas if you walk for
seven or eight hours, you find yourself less hungry, but when you
get to bed you're unexpectedly more up for it—both of you. Perhaps there's a scientific reason for this. Or else the act of reducing
expectation to near zero frees up the libido.

I'm not going to speculate on my parents' sex life. I've no
reason to think it was anything other than what they wanted it
to be—which I realise is a contorted way of putting things. Nor
do I know if they were still happily active, in contented decline,
or if sex for them was an unmourned memory. As I say, my parents held hands whenever they felt like it. They danced together
with a kind of concentrated grace, deliberately old-fashioned.
And I didn't really need an answer to a question I didn't anyway
want to put. Because I'd seen the look in my father's eye when he
talked about not being able to smell his wife. It didn't matter one

way or the other if they were actually having sex. Because their intimacy was still alive.

When Janice and I first got together, we used to head straight back to her place after we'd finished running. She'd tell me to take off my trainers and socks and lie down on the bed while she took a quick shower. Knowing what was coming, I'd usually have a bulge in my shorts by the time she reappeared with a towel wrapped round her. You know how most women have that trick of tucking the towel in just above their breasts with some kind of fold which keeps it all in place? Janice had a different trick: she tucked the towel in just below her breasts.

"Look what's on my bed," she'd say with a twitch of a smile. "What big beast is this on my bed?"

No one had ever called me that before, and I'm just as susceptible to flattery as the next man.

Then she'd kneel on the bed and pretend to inspect me. "What a big sweaty beast we've got here." She'd hold my cock through my shorts and start sniffing at me, at my forehead, then my neck, then my armpits; then she'd pull up my singlet and begin licking my chest and breathing me in, all the while tugging on my cock. The first time it happened, I just came on the spot. Later, I learnt to hold myself back.

And the thing was, she didn't just smell of the shower. She used to put scent on her breasts and hold them above my face.

"Here are your free samples," she'd say.

Then she'd lower a nipple until it was tickling the end of my nose, and tease me by making me guess the name of the perfume. I never knew the answer, but I was in heaven anyway, so I'd usually make up some silly brand instead. You know, Chanel No. 69, that sort of thing.

Speaking of which. Sometimes, after she'd teased my nose,

she'd swivel round above me, and the towel would be gone, and she'd lower herself onto my face, and pull down the top of my shorts. "What've we got here?" she'd say in a carrying whisper. "We've got a big sweaty stinky beast, that's what we've got." And then she'd take my cock in her mouth.

The GP looked up my father's nostrils, and said these things often righted themselves over time. It might just be the after-effect of a virus Dad didn't even know he'd picked up. Give it another six weeks or so. Dad gave it another six weeks, went back, and was given a prescription for some nasal spray. Two squirts up each nostril night and morning. By the end of the course nothing had changed. The doctor offered to refer him to a specialist; naturally, Dad didn't want to bother one.

"It's quite interesting, you know."

"Is it?" I was round at my parents' place, smelling midmorning Nescafé. I didn't believe it could be "interesting" when something went wrong with the body. Painful, irritating, frightening, time-consuming, but not "interesting." That's why I took such care of my own body.

"People think of the obvious things—roses, gravy, beer. But I was never much of a one for smelling roses."

"But if you can't smell, you can't taste, right?"

"That's what they say—that all taste is really smell. But it doesn't seem to apply in my case. I can still taste food and wine the same." He paused. "No, that's not quite right. Some white wines seem more acidic than they used to. I wonder why."

"Is that what's interesting?"

"No. It's the other way round. It's not what you miss, it's what you don't miss. It's a relief not to smell traffic, for instance. You walk past a bus in the market square just sitting there with its engine running, spewing out oily fumes. You'd hold your breath before."

"I'd carry on holding it, Dad." Breathing in noxious fumes without even noticing? The nose was there for a purpose, after all.

"You don't notice the smell of cigarettes, that's another plus. Or the smell of them on someone—I've always hated that. BO, burger vans, Saturday-night vomit on the pavement . . ."

"Dogshit," I suggested.

"Funny you should mention that. It's always made me heave. But I stepped in some the other day and cleaning it off didn't really bother me at all. In the old days I'd have put the shoe outside the back door and left it there for a few days. Oh, and now I cut up onions for Mum. They don't have any effect on me. No tears, nothing. That's a plus."

"That is interesting," I said, half meaning it. Actually, I found it typical of my father's ability to put a positive spin on almost anything. He would have said that examining matters from every point of view was part of his legal habit. I thought him an incorrigible optimist.

"But you know . . . It's things like stepping outside in the morning and sniffing the air. Now I just register whether it's warm or nippy. And furniture polish, I miss that. Shoe polish too. I hadn't thought of it until now. Doing your shoes without being able to smell anything—just imagine it."

I didn't need to, or want to. Coming over all elegiac about tins of Kiwi polish—I hoped I'd never end up like that.

"And, of course, there's your mum."

Yes, my mum.

Both my parents wore glasses, and I sometimes used to imagine them sitting up in bed reading, then putting their book or magazine down, and turning off the bedside light. When did they say good night to one another? Before taking off their glasses or after? Before turning out the light or after? But now I suddenly thought: isn't smell meant to be a central factor in sexual arousal? Pheromones, those primitive things that order us about at the very moment we think we're really in charge. My father com-

plained that he couldn't smell my mother. Perhaps he meant—
had always meant—something more than that.

Jake used to say I had a nose for trouble. With women, he meant.
That's why I was still unmarried at thirty. So are you, I replied.
Yes, but I like it that way, he said. Jake is a big, rangy, curly-haired
fellow who comes on to women in a gentle, unthreatening
manner. It's as if he's saying, Look, I'm here, I'm fun, I'm not
long-term, but you'll probably enjoy me and afterwards we
can still be friends. Quite how he manages to convey such a
complicated message with little more than a grin and a lifted
eyebrow is beyond me. Perhaps it's those pheromones.

Jake's parents split up when he was ten. That's why he's got no
big expectations, he says. Enjoy the day, he says, keep things light.
It's as if he's applied the rules of his running group to the rest of
his life as well. Part of me's impressed by this attitude, but most
of me doesn't want it or envy it.

The first time Janice and I split up, Jake took me to a wine bar,
and while I sipped my daily allowance of a single glass, he told
me, in a sympathetic, roundabout way, how in his opinion she
was untruthful, manipulative and quite possibly psychopathic. I
replied that she was a lively, sexy but complicated girl whom I
sometimes couldn't read, especially at the moment. Jake asked, in
an even more roundabout way, if I realised that she'd come on
to him in the kitchen when he was round to supper three weeks
previously. I told him he was just misreading her friendly manner. That's why she's a psychopath, he replied.

But Jake often called people psychopaths when they were simply more focused than he was, so I didn't take it too much amiss,
and a couple of weeks later Janice and I were back together. In
that first rush of renewed sex and excitement and truthfulness,
I nearly told her what Jake had said, but thought better of it.

Instead, I asked if she'd ever thought of going off with someone else, and she said yes, for about thirty seconds, so I gave her marks for honesty and asked who, and she said no one I knew, and I accepted that, and not long afterwards we got engaged.

I said to my mother, "You do like Janice, don't you?"

"Of course I do. As long as she makes you happy."

"That sounds . . . conditional."

"Well, it is. It would be. A mother's love is unconditional. A mother-in-law's love is conditional. That's how it's always been."

"So if she made me unhappy?"

My mother didn't reply.

"And if I made her unhappy?"

She smiled. "I'd put you across my knee."

As it turned out, we almost didn't get to the wedding. We each postponed once, and even got an official warning from Jake about discussing heavy stuff while out running. When I put it off Janice said it was really because I was scared to commit. When she put it off it was because she wasn't sure about marrying someone who was scared to commit. So somehow it was my fault both times.

One of my father's bridge partners suggested acupuncture. Apparently it had done wonders for the fellow's sciatica.

"But you don't believe in that stuff, Dad."

"I'll believe in it if it cures me," he replied.

"But you're a rationalist, like me."

"We don't have a monopoly of knowledge in the West. Other countries know things too."

"Sure," I agreed. But I felt a kind of alarm, as if things were slipping. We need our parents to remain constant, don't we? And all the more so when we're grown-up ourselves.

"Do you remember—no, you'd've been too young—those

photos of Chinese patients having open-heart surgery? All they had by way of anaesthetic was acupuncture and a copy of Mao's *Little Red Book*."

"What chance those photos were complete fakes?"

"Why should they be?"

"Mao worship. Proof of the superiority of the Chinese way. Also, if it worked, keeping down medical costs."

"You see, you said *if it worked*."

"I didn't mean it."

"You're too cynical, son."

"You're not cynical enough, Dad."

He went to this . . . whatever acupuncturists call their surgery or clinic, in a house on the other side of town. Mrs. Rose wore a white smock, like a nurse or dentist; she was fortyish and sensible-looking, Dad told us. She listened to his story, took his medical details, asked if he suffered from constipation, and explained the principles of Chinese acupuncture. Then she left the room while he stripped to his underpants and lay down under a paper sheet with a blanket on top of it.

"It was all very professional," he reported. "She starts by taking your pulses. In Chinese medicine there are six, three on each side. But the ones on the left wrist are more important because they're for the major organs—heart, liver and kidneys."

I didn't say anything—just felt my alarm growing. And I expect my father read my mood.

"I said to Mrs. Rose, 'I'd better warn you, I'm a bit sceptical,' and she said that didn't matter because acupuncture works whether you believe in it or not."

Except presumably it takes longer with sceptics and so costs more money. I didn't say this either. Instead I let Dad tell us how Mrs. Rose measured his back and marked it up with a felt-tip pen, then put little piles of stuff on his skin and set light to them, and he had to sing out when he felt the heat, and she'd pick them off him. Then there was more measurement and felt-pen markings, and she began sticking needles in him. It was all very hygienic and she dropped the used needles into a sharps box.

At the end of the hour she left the room, and he put his clothes back on and paid her fifty-five pounds. Then he went off to the supermarket to buy dinner. He described standing there in a sort of daze, not knowing what he wanted—or rather, wanting everything he looked at. He wandered around, buying all sorts of stuff, came home in a state of exhaustion, and had to take a nap.

"So you see, it obviously works."

"You mean, you smelt your dinner?"

"No, it's early days—that's only my first treatment. I mean, it clearly has some effect. Both physical and mental."

I thought to myself: feeling tired and buying food you don't need, that sounds like a cure?

"What do you think, Mum?"

"I'm all for him trying something different if he wants to." She reached across the table and patted his arm, near where his mysterious new pulses lay hidden. I needn't have asked—they would have discussed things beforehand and come to a joint conclusion. And as I well knew by now, divide and rule was never successful with my parents.

"If it works, I might try it for my knee," she added.

"What's wrong with your knee, Mum?"

"Oh, I sort of twisted it. I tripped and bashed it on the stairs. I'm getting a bit trippy in my old age."

My mother was fifty-eight. She was wide hipped, with a good, low centre of gravity, and never wore silly shoes.

"You mean, you've done this before?"

"It's nothing. Just age. Comes to us all."

Janice once said that you can never really tell about parents. I asked what she meant. She replied that by the time you were able to understand them, it was too late anyway. You could never find out what they were like before they met, when they met, before you were conceived, afterwards, when you were a small child . . .

"Children often understand a lot," I said. "Instinctively."

"They understand what parents let them understand."

"I don't agree."

"So be it. The point remains. By the time you think you're capable of understanding your parents, most of the important things in their lives have already happened. They are who they are. Or rather, they are who they've decided to be—with you, when you're around."

"I don't agree." I couldn't imagine my parents, once they closed the door, turning into other people.

"How often do you think of your father as a reformed alcoholic?"

"Never. That's not how I think of him. I'm his son, not a social worker."

"Precisely. So you want him to be Just a Dad. No one's just a dad, just a mum. It doesn't work like that. There's probably some secret in your mother's life you've never suspected."

"You'd be laughed out of court," I said.

She looked at me. "I think that what happens with most couples over time is that they find a way of being with one another that is basically untruthful. It's like the relationship depends on mutually assured self-deception. That's its default setting."

"Well, I still don't agree." What I thought was: crap. *Mutually assured self-deception*—that doesn't sound like you. It's some phrase you picked up from that magazine you work for. Or from some bloke you wouldn't mind fucking. But all I said was,

"Are you calling my parents hypocrites?"

"I'm talking generally. Why do you always take things personally?"

"Then I don't understand what you're saying. And if I do, then I can't think why you want to be married to me, or anybody else."

"So be it."

That was another thing. I was beginning to dislike her use of that phrase.

Dad admitted that he hadn't expected acupuncture to hurt as much as it did.

"Do you tell her?"

"Certainly. I say, 'Ow.'"

If Mrs. Rose stuck a needle in and didn't get the reaction she expected, she'd do it again, near the original spot, until she got what she was looking for.

"And what's that?"

"It's a sort of magnetic pull, an energy surge. And you can always tell because that's when it hurts most."

"And then?"

"And then she does it in other places. The backs of the hands, the ankles. That's even more painful—where there isn't much flesh."

"Right."

"But in between she needs to see how your energy levels are coming along, so she's always checking your pulses."

At which point I lost it. "Oh, for Christ's sake, Dad. There's only one pulse, you know that. By definition. It's the pulse of the heart, the pulse of the blood."

My father didn't reply, just cleared his throat slightly and looked at my mother. We don't do rows in our family. We don't want to do them, and we don't know how to, anyway. So there was a silence, and then Mum started on another topic.

Twenty minutes after his fourth treatment, my father walked into Starbucks and smelt coffee for the first time in months. Then he went to the Body Shop to get some shampoo for Mum, and said it was like being hit over the head by a rhododendron bush. He was almost nauseous. The smells were so rich, he said, that it was as if they had bright colours attached to them as well.

"So what do you say about that?"

"I don't know what to say, Dad, except congratulations." I thought it was probably coincidence or autosuggestion.

"You're not going to pretend it's a coincidence?"

"No, Dad, I'm not."

Mrs. Rose, to his surprise, greeted his account neutrally, with a little head nodding and some scribbling in a notebook. She then explained her proposed course of action. There would, if he agreed, be fortnightly appointments building towards the summer—by which she meant the Chinese, not the British, summer, because that, based on my father's date of birth, would be his time of maximum responsiveness. She added that his energy levels were rising every time she checked his pulses.

"Do you feel more energetic, Dad?"

"That's not what it's about."

"And have you smelt anything since your last appointment?"

"No."

Right, so "energy levels" had nothing to do with "levels of energy," and having higher ones didn't increase his smelling power. Fine.

Sometimes I wondered why I was being so hard on my father. Over the next three months he reported his findings matter-of-factly. From time to time he smelt things, but they had to be strong to get through: soap, coffee, burnt toast, toilet cleaner; twice, a glass of red wine; once, to his joy, the smell of rain. The Chinese summer came and went; Mrs. Rose said that acupuncture had done all it could. My father, typically, blamed his own scepticism, but Mrs. Rose repeated that attitude of mind was irrelevant. Since she was the one who proposed ending the treatment, I decided that she wasn't a charlatan. But perhaps it was more that I didn't want to think of Dad as the sort of person who could be taken in by a charlatan.

"Actually, it's your mother I'm more worried about."

"Why's that?"

"She seems, I don't know, a bit off the pace nowadays. Maybe it's just tiredness. She's slower, somehow."

"What does she say?"

"Oh, she says there's nothing wrong. Or if there is, it's just hormonal."

"What does she mean?"

"I was rather hoping you could tell me."

That was another nice thing about my parents. There was none of that holding on to knowledge and power that some parents go in for. We were all adults together, on a plateau of equality.

"I probably don't know any better than you, Dad. But in my experience, 'hormones' is a catchall word for when women don't want to tell you something. I always think: hang on, haven't men got hormones as well? Why don't we use them as an excuse?"

My father chuckled, but I could see his anxiety wasn't allayed. So on his next bridge night, I dropped in on Mum. As we sat in the kitchen, I could tell immediately that she hadn't bought my excuse of "just being in the neighbourhood."

"Tea or coffee?"

"Decaf or herbal tea, whatever you're having."

"Well, I need a good dose of caffeine."

Somehow, it didn't take more than that to bring me to the point.

"Dad's worried about you. So am I."

"Dad's a worrier."

"Dad loves you. That's why he notices things about you. If he didn't, he wouldn't."

"No, I suppose that's right." I looked at her, but her gaze was elsewhere. It was perfectly clear to me that she was thinking about being loved. It could have made me feel envious, but it didn't.

"So tell me what's wrong, and don't mention hormones."

She smiled. "A bit tired. A bit clumsy. That's all."


About eighteen months into the marriage, Janice accused me of not being straightforward. Of course, being Janice, she didn't put it as straightforwardly as that. She asked why I always preferred discussing unimportant problems rather than important ones. I said I didn't think this was so, but in any case, big things are sometimes so big that there's little to say about them, whereas small things are easier to discuss. And sometimes we think this is the problem, whereas it's actually that, which makes this seem trivial. She looked at me like one of my stroppier pupils, and said that was typical—a typical justification of my natural evasiveness, my refusal to face facts and deal with issues. She said she could always smell a lie on me. She actually put it like that.

"Very well, then," I replied. "Let's be straightforward. Let's deal with issues. You're having an affair and I'm having an affair. Is that facing facts or not?"

"That's what you think it is. You make it sound like a one-all draw." And then she explained the falseness of my apparent candour, and the difference between our infidelities—hers born of despair, mine of revenge—and how it was symptomatic that I thought the affairs were the significant thing, rather than the circumstances which gave rise to them. And so we came full circle to the original charges.

What do we look for in a partner? Someone like us, someone different? Someone like us but different, different but like us? Someone to complete us? Oh, I know you can't generalise, but even so. The point is: if we're looking for someone who matches us, we only ever think of their good matching bits. What about their bad matching bits? Do you think we're sometimes driven towards people with the same faults as we have?

My mother. When I think of her now, there's a phrase that comes to mind—one I used when Dad was rabbiting on about his six Chinese pulses. Dad, I said to him, there's only one pulse—the pulse of the heart, the pulse of the blood. The photographs of my parents that I'm most attached to are those taken before I was born. And—thank you, Janice—I do actually think I know what they were like back then.

My parents sitting on a pebble beach somewhere, his arm around her shoulders; he has a sports jacket with leather elbow patches, she's in a polka-dot dress, looking out at the camera with passionate hopefulness. My parents on their honeymoon in Spain, with mountains behind them, both wearing sunglasses, so you have to work out how they're feeling from their stance, their obvious relaxation with one another, and the sly fact that my mother has her hand slipped into my father's trouser pocket. And then a picture which must have meant a lot to them despite its shortcomings: the two of them at a party, clearly more than a bit drunk, with the camera flash giving them the pink eyes of white mice. My father has absurd muttonchop whiskers, Mum frizzy hair, big hoop earrings and a kaftan. Neither looks as if they could possibly grow up enough to be a parent. I suspect this is the first picture ever taken of them together, the first time they are officially recorded as sharing the same space, breathing the same air.

There's also a photo on the sideboard of me with my parents. I'm about four or five, standing between them with the expression of a child who's been told to watch the birdie, or however they might have put it: concentrating, but at the same time not quite certain of what's going on. I'm holding a junior watering can, though I have no memory of being given a junior gardener's kit, or indeed of having any interest, real or suggested, in gardening.

Nowadays, when I examine this photo—my mother looking down at me protectively, my father smiling at the camera, a drink in one hand and a cigarette in the other—I can't help remembering Janice's words. About how parents decide who they are before the child has any awareness of it, how they develop a front which the child will never be able to penetrate. Whether intentional or not, there was something poisonous in her remarks. "You want him to be Just a Dad. No one's just a dad, just a mum." And then: "There's probably some secret in your mother's life you've never suspected." What am I to do with that thought? Even if I were to pursue it and find it led nowhere?

There's nothing mimsy or flaky about my mum and nothing—note this, please, Janice—nothing neurotically self-dramatising. She's a solid presence in a room, whether talking or not. And she's the person you would turn to if anything went wrong. Once, when I was little, she managed to gash herself in the thigh. There was no one else in the house. Most people would have called an ambulance, or at least disturbed Dad at his work. But Mum just got a needle and some surgical thread, pulled the wound together and sewed it up. And she'd do the same for you without turning a hair. That's what she's like. If there is a secret in her life, it's probably that she helped someone and never told anybody about it. So fuck Janice, is what I say.

My parents met when Dad had just qualified as a solicitor. He used to maintain that he'd had to chase off a number of rivals. Mum said there wasn't any chasing to be done because everything was perfectly obvious to her from the day they met. Yes, Dad would reply, but the other fellows didn't see it that way. My mother would look at him fondly, and I could never work out which of them to believe. Or perhaps that's the definition of a happy marriage: both parties are telling the truth, even when their accounts are incompatible.

Of course, my admiration for their marriage is partly conditioned by the failure of my own. Perhaps their example made me assume it was more straightforward than it turned out. Do you think there are people who have a talent for marriage, or is it just a question of luck? Though I suppose you could say that it's luck to have such a talent. When I mentioned to Mum that Janice and I were going through a bad patch and trying to work at our marriage, she said,

"I've never really understood what that means. If you love your job, it doesn't feel like work. If you love your marriage, it doesn't feel like work. I suppose you may be working at it, underneath. Just doesn't feel like it," she repeated. And then, after a pause, "Not that I'm saying anything against Janice."

"Let's not talk about Janice," I said. I'd already talked enough about Janice to Janice herself. Whatever we brought to that marriage, we sure as hell took nothing away from it, except our legal share of money.

You would think, wouldn't you, that if you were the child of a happy marriage, then you ought to have a better than average marriage yourself—either through some genetic inheritance or because you'd learnt from example? But it doesn't seem to work like that. So perhaps you need the opposite example—to see mistakes in order not to make them yourself. Except this would mean that the best way for parents to ensure their children have happy marriages would be to have unhappy ones themselves. So what's the answer? I don't know. Only that I don't blame my parents; nor, really, do I blame Janice.

My mother promised that she would go to their GP if Dad saw a specialist about his anosmia. My father was typically reluctant. Others had it far worse than him, he said. He could still taste his food, whereas for some anosmiacs dinner was like chewing card-board and plastic. He'd been on the Internet and read about even more extreme cases—for instance, of olfactory hallucination. Imagine if fresh milk suddenly smelt and tasted sour, chocolate made you retch, meat was just like a sponge of blood to you.

"If you dislocate your finger," my mother replied, "you don't refuse to get it looked at because someone else has broken their leg."

And so the bargain was made. The waiting and the bureau-cracy began, and they both ended up having MRI scans in the same week. What are the chances of that, I wonder.

I'm not sure we ever know exactly when our marriage ends. We remember certain stages, transitions, arguments, incompatibilities which grow until they can't be resolved or lived with. I think that for much of the time when Janice was attacking me—or, as she would put it, the time when I stopped paying attention to her and just went missing—I never really thought this was, or would cause, the end of our marriage. It was only when, for no reason I could comprehend, she turned on my parents that I first began to think: oh really, now she's crossed the line. It's true, we'd been drinking. And yes, I had exceeded my self-imposed limit—well exceeded it.

"One of your problems is, you think your parents have the perfect marriage."

"Why is that one of my problems?"

"Because it makes you think your marriage is worse than it is."

"Oh, so it's their fault, is it?"

"No, they're fine, your parents."

"But?"

"I said they're fine. I just didn't say the sun shines out of their arses."

"You don't think the sun shines out of anyone's arse, do you?"

"Well, it doesn't. But I like your dad, he's always been nice to me."

"Meaning?"

"Meaning, mothers and only sons. Do I have to spell it out?"

"I think you just did."

A few weeks later, one Saturday afternoon, Mum phoned in a bit of a fluster. She'd driven to an antiques fair in a nearby town to get Dad a birthday present, had a puncture on the way back, managed to get the car to the nearest petrol station, only to find—none too surprisingly—that the cashiers wouldn't leave their tills. They probably didn't know how to change a wheel anyway. Dad had said he was going to have a lie-down and—

"Don't worry, Mum, I'll be along. Ten, fifteen minutes." I didn't have anything else to do. But before I could hang up, Janice, who'd been monitoring my end of the conversation, shouted across at me,

"Why can't she call the fucking AA or RAC?"

It was obvious that Mum would have heard, and that this was what Janice had intended.

I put the phone down. "You can come too," I said to her. "And lie under the car while I jack it up." As I fetched the car keys, I thought to myself: right, that's it.

Most people don't like to bother their doctor. But most people don't like the idea of being ill. And most people don't want to be accused, even implicitly, of wasting the doctor's time. So in theory, going to the doctor is a win-win situation: either you come out confirmed as healthy, or else it's true that you haven't been wasting the doctor's time. My father, his scan revealed, had a chronic sinus condition for which he was prescribed antibiotics followed by more nasal spray; beyond that lay the possibility of an operation. My mother, after blood tests, EMG and MRI, and then a process of elimination, was diagnosed with motor neuron disease.

"You'll look after your father, won't you?"

"Of course, Mum," I replied, not knowing if she meant the short term or the long term. And I expect she had a similar exchange with Dad about me.

My father said, "Look at Stephen Hawking. He's had it for forty years." I suspect he'd been on the same website as I had; from which he would also have learnt that 50 percent of MND sufferers die within fourteen months.

Dad was incensed by the way they handled it at the hospital. No sooner had the specialist explained his conclusions than they took Mum and Dad down to some supply room and showed them the wheelchairs and stuff which would become necessary as her condition inevitably deteriorated. Dad said it was like being taken to a torture dungeon. He was very upset, for Mum's sake mainly, I think. She took it all calmly, he said. But then she'd worked at that hospital for fifteen years, and knew what its rooms contained.

I found it hard to talk to Dad about what was happening—and he to me. I kept thinking: Mum's dying, but Dad's losing her. I felt that if I repeated the phrase enough times, it would make sense. Or stop it happening. Or something. I also thought: Mum's the one we turn to when anything goes wrong; so who do we turn to when something goes wrong with her? In the meantime—waiting for the answers—Dad and I discussed her daily needs: who was looking after her, how her spirits were, what she'd said, and the question of medication (or rather, the lack of it, and whether we should push for Riluzole). We could, and did, discuss such matters endlessly. But the catastrophe itself—its suddenness, whether we might have seen it coming, how much Mum had been covering up, the prognosis, the unavoidable outcome—these we could only hint at from time to time. Perhaps we were just too exhausted. We needed to talk about normal English things, like the probable effect on local businesses of the proposed ring road. Or I would ask Dad about his anosmia and we would both pretend it was still an interesting subject. The antibiotics had worked at first, making smells come back in a rush; but soon—after about three days—the effect wore off. Dad, being Dad, didn't tell me at the time; he said it felt like an irrelevant joke, given what was happening to Mum.

I read somewhere that those who are close to someone who's seriously ill often take to doing crossword puzzles or jigsaws in their hours away from the hospital. For one thing, they don't have the concentration for anything more serious; but there's also another reason. Consciously or unconsciously, they need to work at something with rules, laws, answers, and an overall solution; something fixable. Of course, illness has its laws and rules and sometimes its answers, but that's not how you experience it at the bedside. And then there's the remorselessness of hope. Even when hope of cure is gone, there is hope for other things—some specific, others not. Hope means uncertainty, and persists even when you've been told there is only one answer, one certainty— the single, unacceptable one.

I didn't do crosswords or jigsaws—I don't have that sort of mind, or patience. But I became more obsessive about my exer- cise programme. I lifted more weights and increased my time on the step machine. On Friday runs, I found myself at the front of the pack, with the heavy guys who don't do chat. That suited me fine. I wore my heart monitor, checked my pulse, consulted my watch, and occasionally I talked of the calories I'd done. I ended up fitter than I'd been at any time in my life. And sometimes— crazy as it may sound—that felt like solving something.

I sublet my flat and moved back in with my parents. I knew Mum would be against the idea—for my sake, not hers—so I merely presented her with the fait accompli. Dad took a leave of absence from his office; I cut out all extracurricular activities; we called in friends, and later nurses. The house sprouted handrails, then wheelchair ramps. Mum moved downstairs; Dad never spent a night apart from her, until she went to the hospice. I remember it as a time of absolute panic, but also a time with a rigorous daily logic to it. You followed the logic, and that seemed to hold the panic at bay.

Mum was amazing. I know MND sufferers are statistically less likely to be depressed about their condition than patients with other degenerative illnesses, but even so. She didn't pretend to be braver than she was; she wasn't afraid to cry in front of us; she didn't make jokes to try and cheer us up. She treated what was happening to her soberly, without flinching from it or letting it overwhelm her—this thing that was going to crush out her senses one by one. She talked herself—and us—through her life and our lives. She never referred to Janice, or said she hoped I'd eventually have her grandchildren. She didn't lay anything on us, or make us promise stuff for afterwards. There was a stage when she weakened dramatically and every breath sounded like a hike up Everest; then I wondered if she was thinking about that place in Switzerland where you can make a decent end to it all. But I dismissed the thought: she wouldn't want to put us to such bother. This was another sign that she was—as far as she could be—in charge of her own dying. She was the one who made sure the hospice was lined up, and told us it was better to move sooner rather than later, because you could never predict when places became free.

The bigger the matter, the less there is to say. Not to *feel*, but to say. Because there is only the fact itself, and your feelings about the fact. Nothing else. My father, faced with his anosmia, could find reasons why such a disadvantage might, if viewed from the right perspective, become an advantage. But Mum's illness was in a category way beyond this, beyond rationality; it was something enormous, mute and muting. There was no counterargument. Nor was it a matter of not being able to find the words. The words are always there—and they are always the same words, simple words. Mum's dying, but Dad's losing her. I always said it with a "but" in the middle, never an "and."

I was surprised to get a call from Janice.

"I'm very sorry to hear about your mother."

"Yes."

"Is there anything I can do?"

"Who did you hear from?"

"Jake."

"You're not seeing Jake, are you?"

"I'm not seeing-seeing Jake, if that's what you're asking." But she said it in a frisky tone, as if excited that she might, even now, be provoking a stir of jealousy.

"No, I'm not asking."

"Except that you just did."

Same old Janice, I thought. "Thank you for your sympathy," I said, as formally as I could. "No, there's nothing you can do, and no, she wouldn't like a visit."

"So be it."

The summer Mum was dying was hot, and Dad wore those short-sleeved shirts of his. He used to wash them by hand, then struggle with the steam iron. One evening, when I could see he was exhausted, and trying unsuccessfully to fit the yoke of a shirt across the pointy end of the ironing board, I said,

"You could send them to the laundry, you know."

He didn't look at me, just carried on wrenching at the damp shirt.

"I am well aware," he eventually replied, "that such businesses exist." Mild sarcasm from my father had the force of rage from anyone else.

"Sorry, Dad."

Then he did stop and look at me. "It's very important," he said, "that she sees me looking neat and tidy. If I started getting scruffy, she'd notice, and she'd think I couldn't manage. And she mustn't think I can't manage. Because that would upset her."

"Yes, Dad." I felt rebuked; I felt, for once, a child.

Later, he came and sat with me. I had a beer, he had a careful whisky. Mum had been in the hospice three days. She had seemed calm that evening, and packed us off with no more than the switch of an eye.

"By the way," he said, settling his glass on a coaster, "I'm sorry your mother didn't like Janice." We both heard the tense of the verb. "Doesn't," he inserted into the sentence, far too late.

"I never knew that."

"Ah." My father paused. "Sorry. Nowadays . . ." He didn't need to go on.

"Why not?"

His mouth tightened, as I imagine it did when a client told him something unwise—like, Yes, I was at the scene of the crime after all.

"Come on, Dad. Was it because of the garage incident? The puncture."

"What puncture?"

So she hadn't told him that.

"I always rather liked Janice. She was . . . sparky."

"Yes, Dad. The point."

"Your mother said she thought Janice was the sort of girl who knew how to make people feel guilty."

"Yes, she was particularly good at that."

"She used to complain to your mother about how difficult you were to live with—somehow implying that it was your mother's fault."

"She ought to have been grateful. I'd have been a lot harder to live with if it hadn't been for Mum's love." Once again, a mistake born of tiredness. "Both of you, I mean."

My father didn't take the correction amiss. He sipped his drink.

"So what else, Dad?"

"Isn't that enough?"

"I just think you're holding something back."

My father smiled. "Yes, you might have made a lawyer. Well, this was towards the end of—of your . . . when Janice was hardly herself."

"So spit it out and we'll laugh at it together."

"She told your mother she thought you were a bit of a psychopath."

I may have smiled, but I didn't laugh.


We saw so many different people at the hospital and the hospice that I can no longer remember who told us that when someone is dying, when the whole system is shutting down, the last remaining senses still at work are usually those of hearing and smell. My mother was by now quite immobile, and being turned every four hours. She hadn't talked for a week, and her eyes were no longer open. She had made it clear that when her swallow reflex weakened, she didn't want a gastric feed. The dying body can exist for long enough without the sludge of nutrients they like to pump into it.

My father told me how he went to the supermarket and bought various packets of fresh herbs. At the hospice he closed the curtains round the bed. He didn't want others to see this intimate moment. He wasn't embarrassed—my father was never embarrassed by his uxoriousness—he just wanted his privacy. Their privacy.

I imagine them together, my father sitting on the bed, kissing my mother, not knowing if she could feel it, talking to her, not knowing if she could hear his words, nor, even if she could, whether she could understand them. He had no way of knowing, she no way of telling him.

I imagine him worrying about the ripping noise as he opened the plastic sachets, and what she might think was happening. I imagine him solving the problem by taking a pair of scissors with him to cut open the packets. I imagine him explaining that he had brought some herbs for her to smell. I imagine him rubbing basil into a roll beneath her nostrils. I imagine him crushing thyme between finger and thumb, then rosemary. I imagine him naming them, and believing she could smell them, and hoping that they would bring her pleasure, would remind her of the world and the delight she had taken in it—perhaps even of some occasion on a foreign hillside or scrubland when their shoes tramped out a rising scent of wild thyme. I imagine him hoping that the smells wouldn't come as a terrible mockery, reminding her of the sun she could no longer see, gardens she could no longer walk in, aromatic food she could no longer enjoy.

I hope he didn't imagine these last things; I hope he was convinced that in her last days she was granted only the best, the happiest thoughts.

A month after my mother died, my father had his last appointment with the ENT specialist.

"He said he could operate, but couldn't promise more than a sixty/forty success rate. I told him I didn't want an operation. He said he was loath to give up on my case, especially since my anosmia was only partial. He thought my sense of smell was waiting there and could be brought back."

"How?"

"More of the same. Antibiotics, nasal spray. Slightly different prescription. I told him thanks but no thanks."

"Right." I didn't say any more. It was his decision.

"You see, if your mother . . ."

"It's all right, Dad."

"No, it's not all right. If she . . ."

I looked at him, at the tears pent up behind the lenses of his spectacles, then released to run down his cheeks to his jaw. He let them run; he was used to them; they didn't bother him. Nor did they bother me.

He started again. "If she . . . Then I don't . . ."

"Sure, Dad."

"I think it helps, in a kind of way."

"Sure, Dad."

He lifted his glasses from the creases of flesh in which they sat, and the last tears ran down the sides of his nose. He wiped the back of a hand across his cheeks.

"You know what that buggery specialist said to me when I told him I didn't want an operation?"

"No, Dad."

"He sat there meditating for a bit and then said, 'Do you have a smoke alarm?' I told him we didn't. He said, 'You might be able to get the council to pay for it. Out of their disability funds.' I said I didn't know about that. Then he went on, 'But I suppose I'd advise a top-of-the-range number, and they might not be willing to cover the cost.'"

"Sounds a pretty surreal conversation."

"It was. Then he said he didn't like to think of me being asleep and only realising the house was on fire when I was woken by the heat."

"Did you punch him, Dad?"

"No, son. I got up, shook him by the hand, and said, 'That would be one solution, I suppose.'"

I imagine my father there, not getting angry, standing up, shaking hands, turning, leaving. I imagine it.

# ALSO BY JULIAN BARNES

### ARTHUR AND GEORGE

As boys, George, the son of a Midlands vicar, and Arthur, living in shabby-genteel Edinburgh, find themselves in a vast and complex world at the heart of the British Empire. Years later—one struggling with an identity in a world hostile to his ancestry, and the other creating the world's most famous detective—their fates become inextricably connected.

Fiction/Literature

### BEFORE SHE MET ME

At the start of this novel, an English academic chuckles as he watches his wife commit adultery in a silly, low-budget movie she made years before she met him. But as he combs the theaters for other instances of his wife's cinematic betrayal, the line between film and reality, past and present, love and mania becomes terrifyingly blurred.

Fiction/Literature

### ENGLAND, ENGLAND

Imagine an England in which all the pubs are quaint, the Windsors behave themselves (mostly), and the cliffs of Dover are actually white, and where Robin Hood and his merry men really are merry. This is precisely what visionary tycoon Sir Jack Pitman seeks to accomplish on the Isle of Wight, a "destination" where tourists can find replicas of Big Ben (half size), Princess Di's grave, and even Harrod's.

Fiction/Literature

### FLAUBERT'S PARROT

An elegant work of literary imagination involving a cranky, erudite amateur scholar's obsessive search for the truth about Gustave Flaubert, *Flaubert's Parrot* also investigates the scholar himself, whose passion for the page is fed by personal bitterness—and whose life seems oddly to mirror those of Flaubert's characters.

Fiction/Literature

## A HISTORY OF THE WORLD IN 10½ CHAPTERS

Beginning with a revisionist account of the voyage of Noah's ark (narrated by one of its passengers) and ending with a sneak preview of heaven, Julian Barnes's tour de force is a complete, unsettling, and frequently exhilarating vision of the world.

Fiction/Literature

## THE LEMON TABLE

In his acclaimed collection of stories, Barnes addresses what is perhaps the most poignant aspect of the human condition: growing old. The characters are facing the ends of their lives—some with bitter regret, others with resignation, and others still with defiant rage.

Fiction/Short Stories

## LETTERS FROM LONDON

Formidably articulate and outrageously funny, *Letters from London* is international voyeurism at its best—a peek into the British mindset from the vantage point of one of the most erudite and witty British minds.

Literature/Nonfiction

ALSO AVAILABLE
*Love, Etc.*
*Metroland*
*Nothing to Be Frightened of*
*The Porcupine*
*Something to Declare*
*Staring at the Sun*
*Talking It Over*
*Cross Channel*

VINTAGE INTERNATIONAL
Available wherever books are sold.
www.randomhouse.com